pocket.watch

RYAN'S WORLD™

RED TITAN
AND THE NEVER-ENDING MAZE

SIMON SPOTLIGHT

An imprint of Simon & Schuster Children's Publishing Division
1230 Avenue of the Americas, New York, New York 10020
This Simon Spotlight edition December 2021
Text by Arie Kaplan

For more information about special discounts for bulk purchases, please contact
Simon & Schuster Special Sales at 1-866-506-1949 or business@simonandschuster.com.
Manufactured in the United States of America 1122 LAK
2 4 6 8 10 9 7 5 3
ISBN 978-1-6659-0182-6 (hc)
ISBN 978-1-6659-0181-9 (pbk)
ISBN 978-1-6659-0183-3 (ebook)

RED TITAN

AND THE NEVER-ENDING MAZE

by **RYAN KAJI**
written by **ARIE KAPLAN**
illustrated by **SHANE L. JOHNSON**

Ready-to-Read *GRAPHICS*

Simon Spotlight
New York London Toronto Sydney New Delhi

HOW TO READ THIS BOOK

Ryan is here to give you some tips on reading this book.

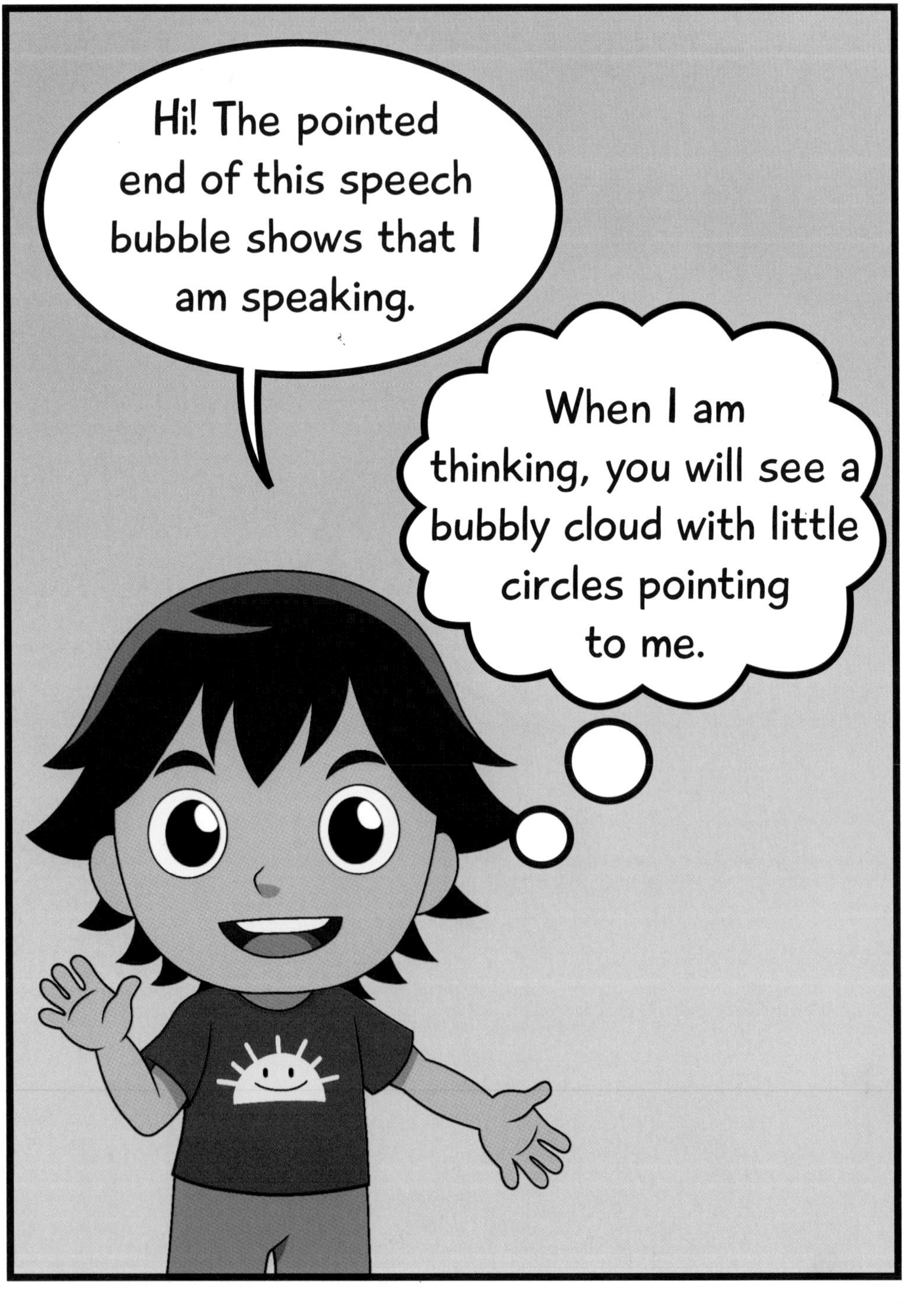
Hi! The pointed end of this speech bubble shows that I am speaking.
When I am thinking, you will see a bubbly cloud with little circles pointing to me.

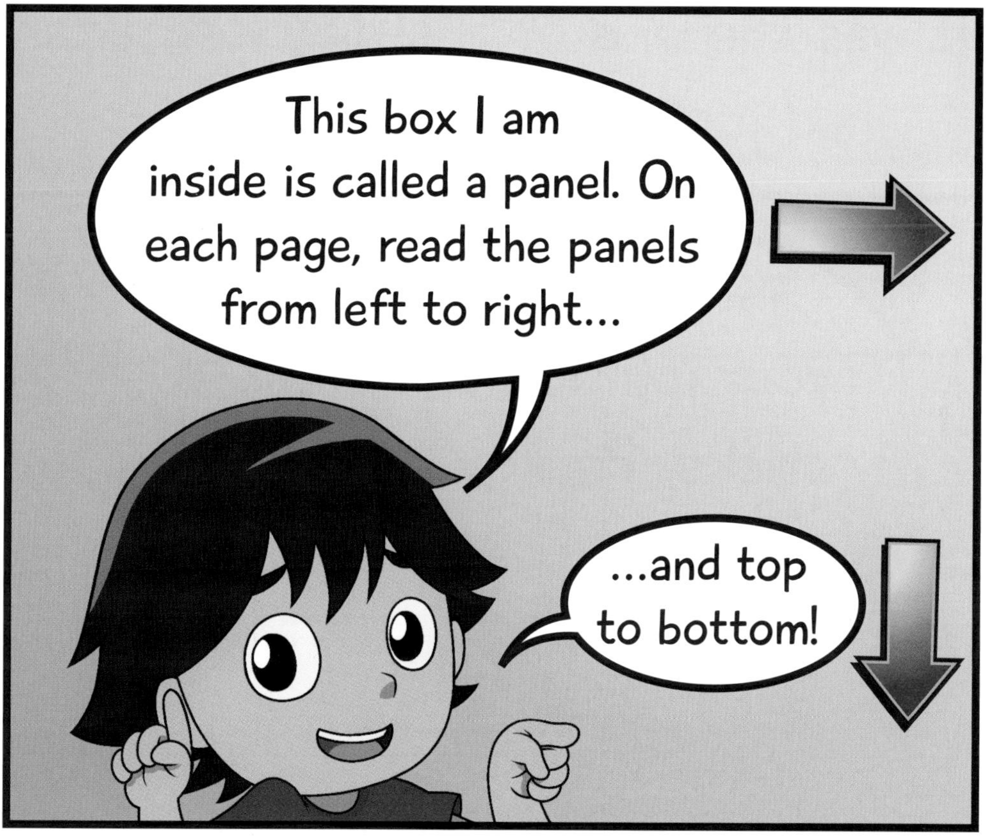
This box I am inside is called a panel. On each page, read the panels from left to right...
...and top to bottom!

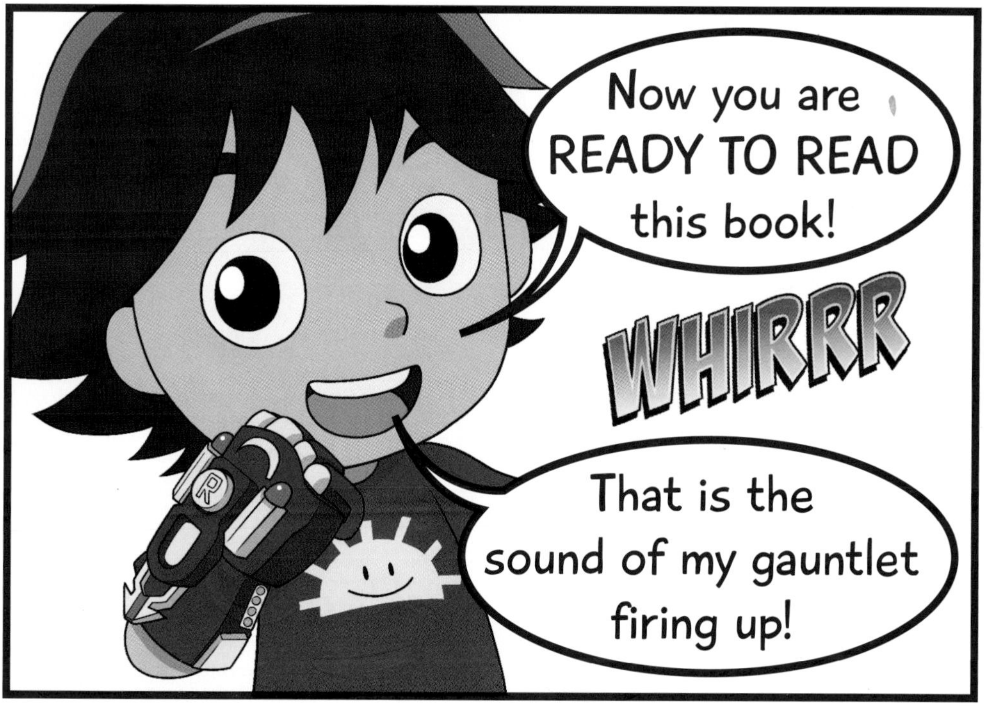
Now you are READY TO READ this book!
WHIRRR
That is the sound of my gauntlet firing up!

It was the end of the day. Red Titan had just finished his last job.

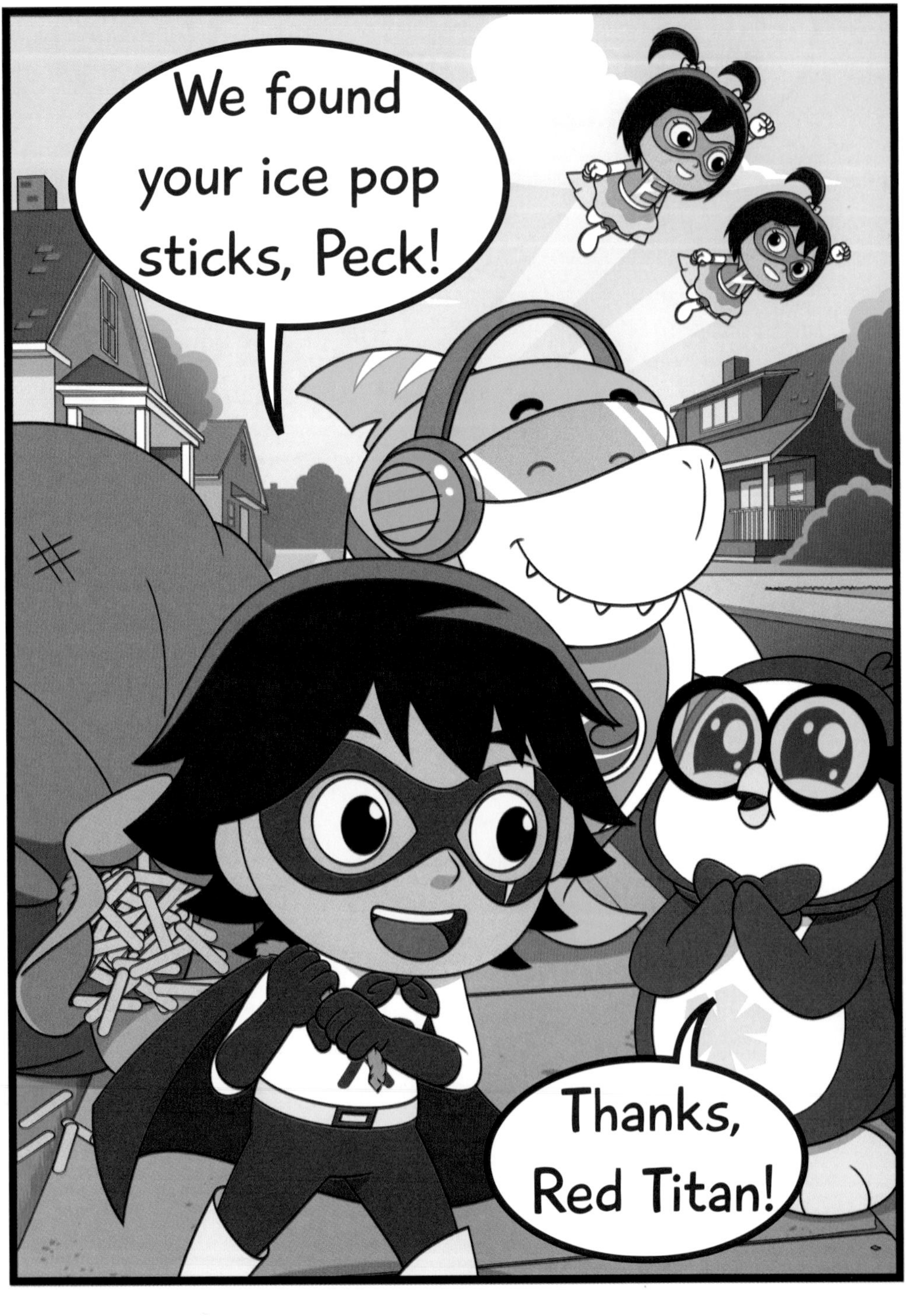
We found your ice pop sticks, Peck!
Thanks, Red Titan!

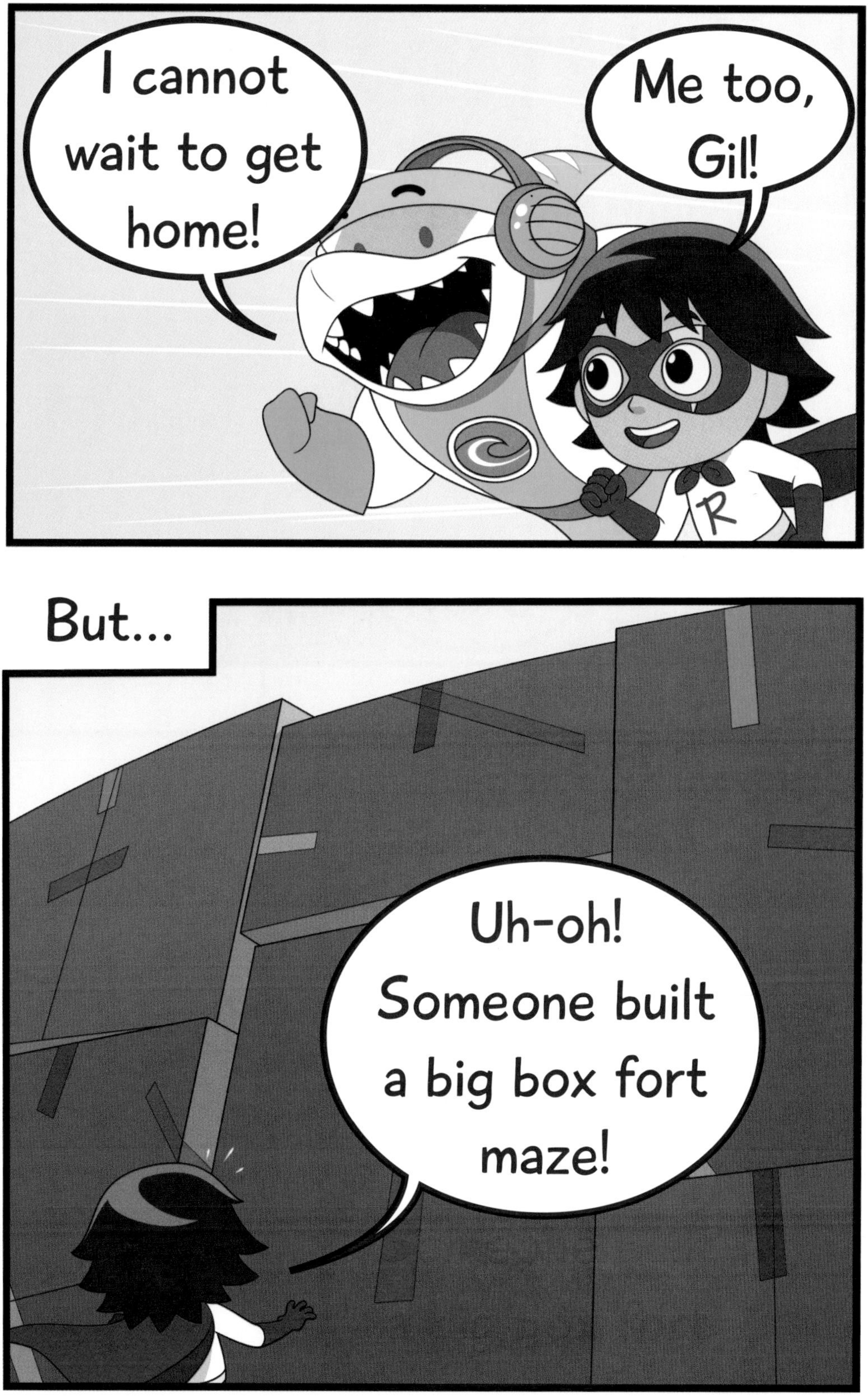
I cannot wait to get home!
Me too, Gil!
But...
Uh-oh! Someone built a big box fort maze!

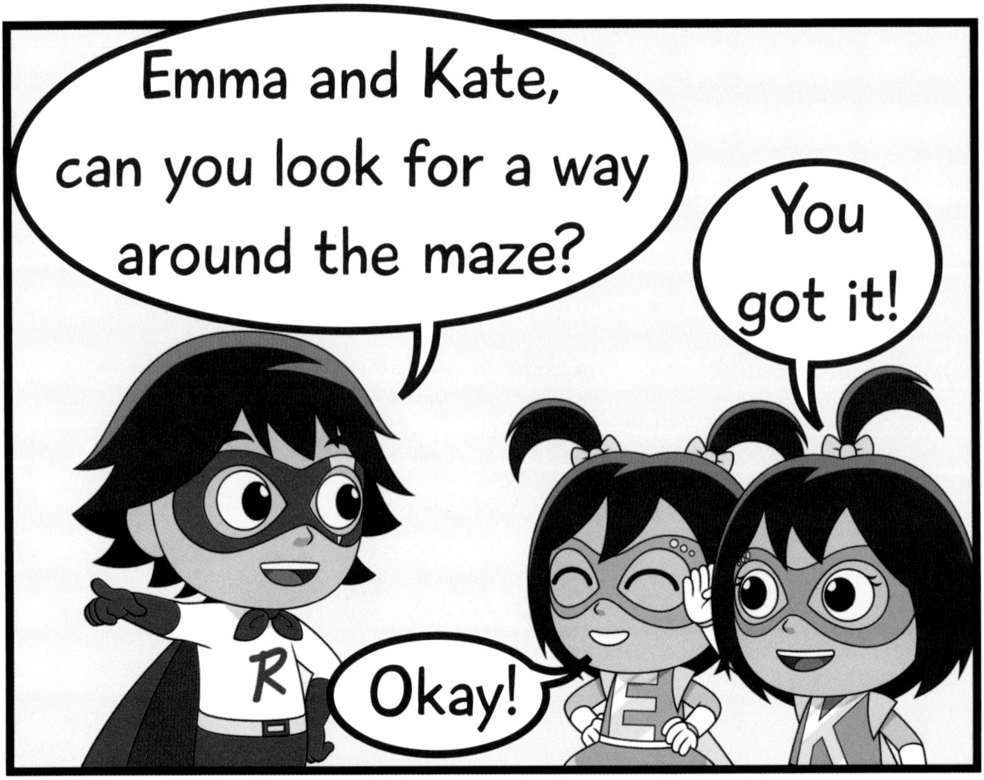
Emma and Kate, can you look for a way around the maze?
You got it!
Okay!

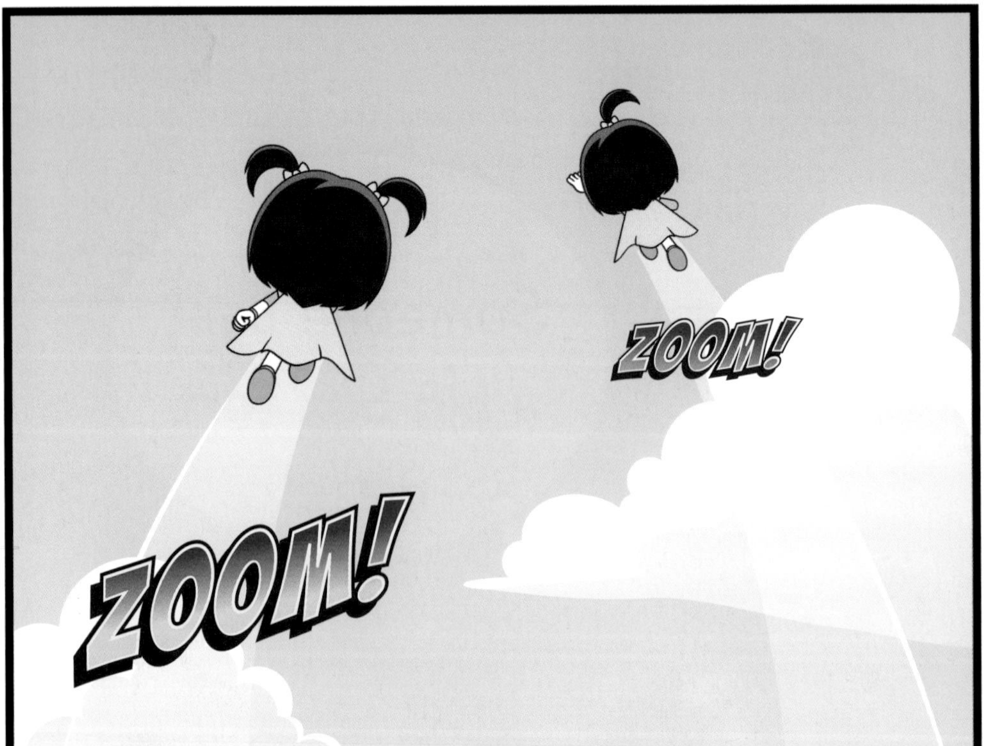
ZOOM!
ZOOM!

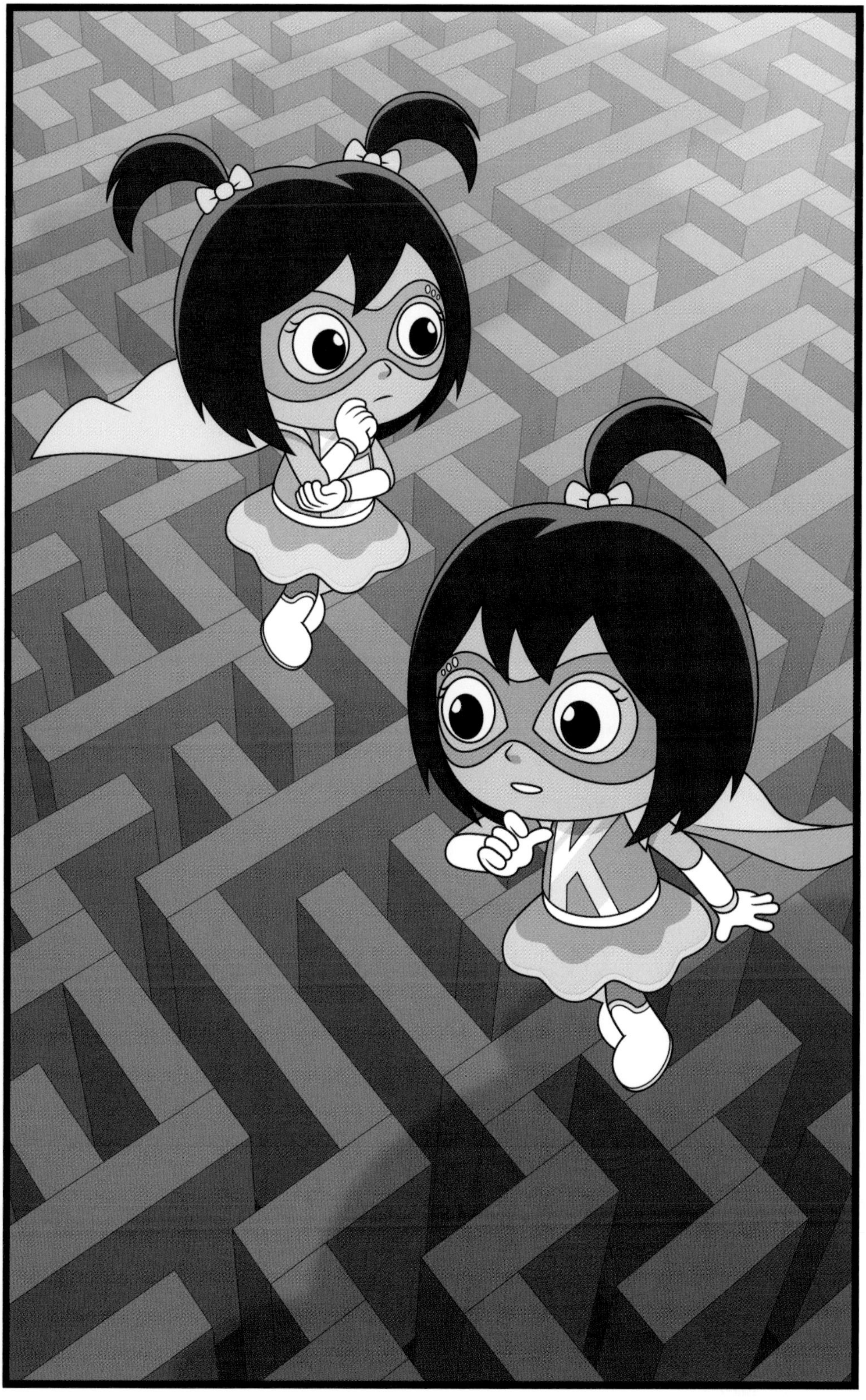

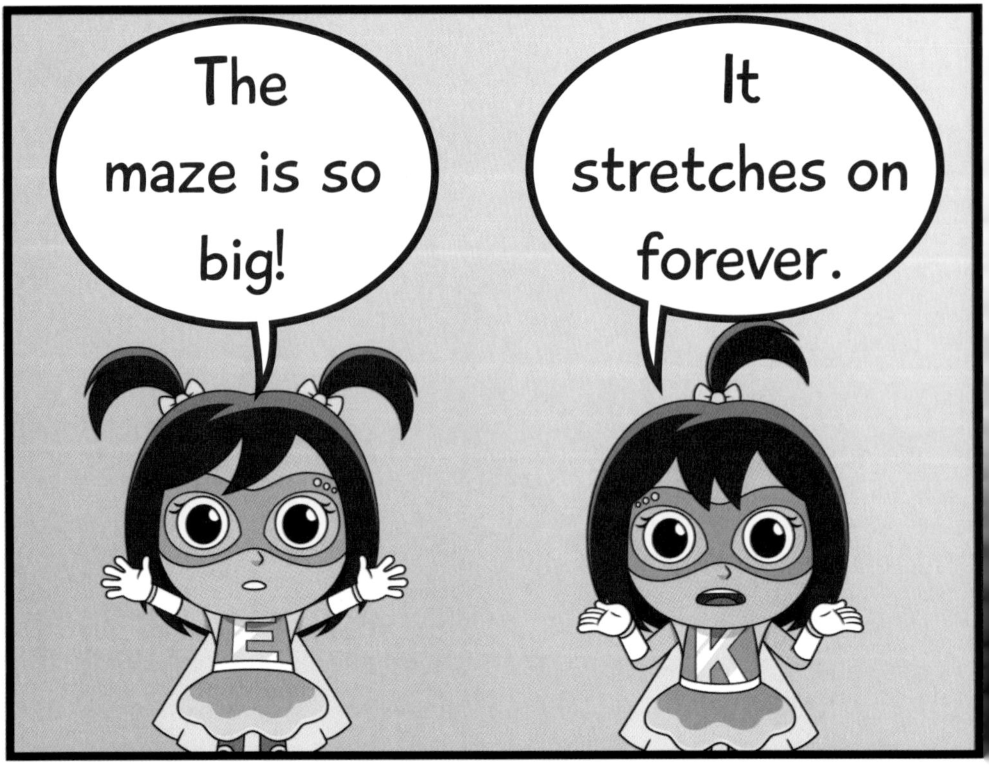
The maze is so big!
It stretches on forever.

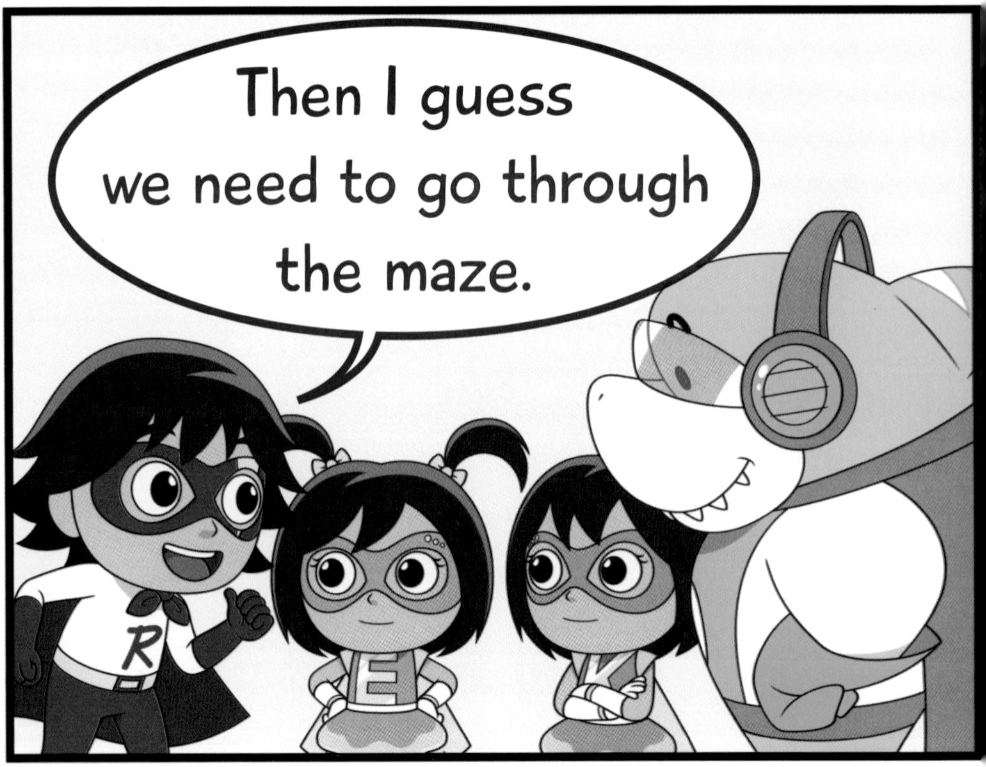
Then I guess we need to go through the maze.

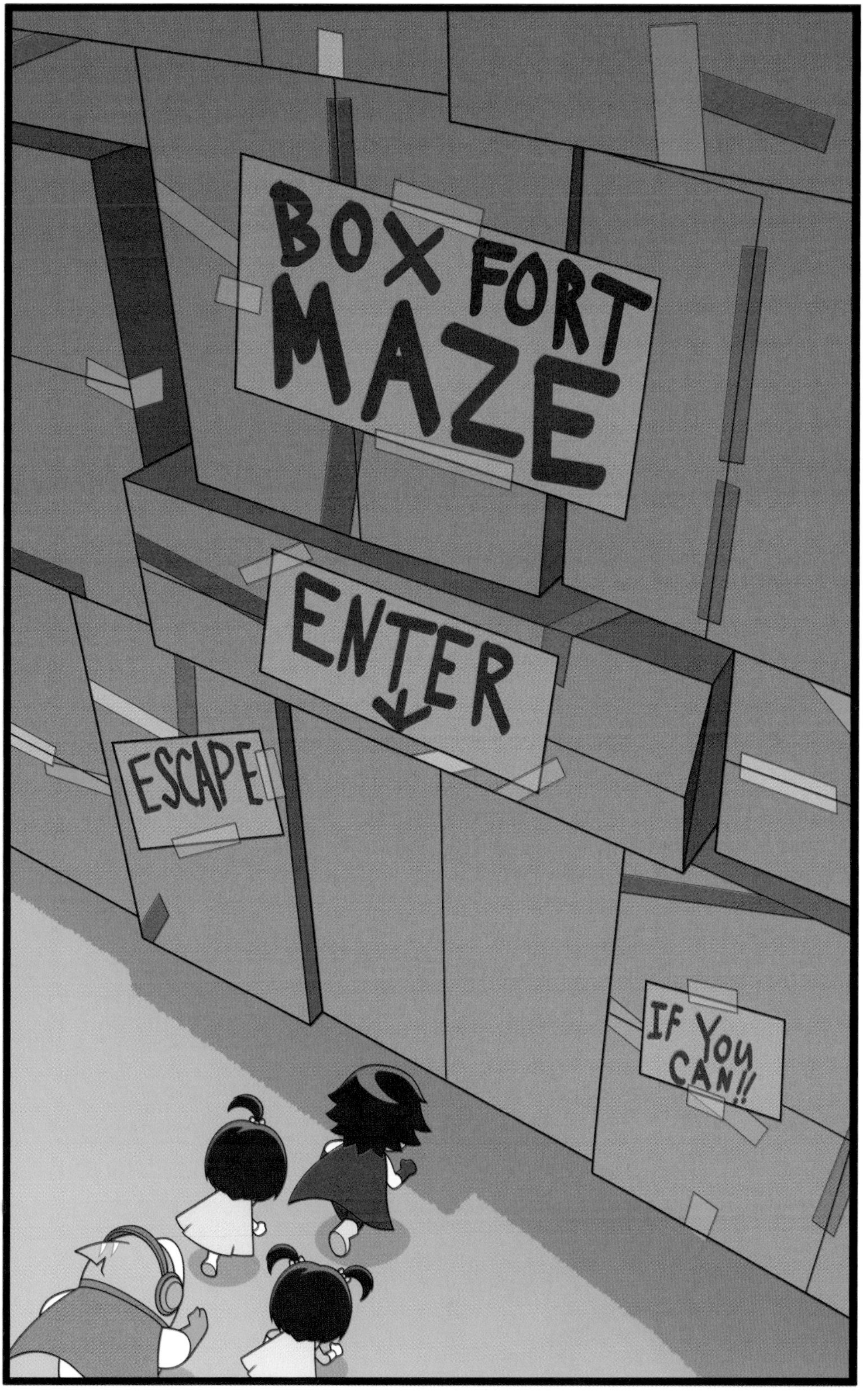
BOX FORT MAZE
ENTER
ESCAPE
IF YOU CAN!!

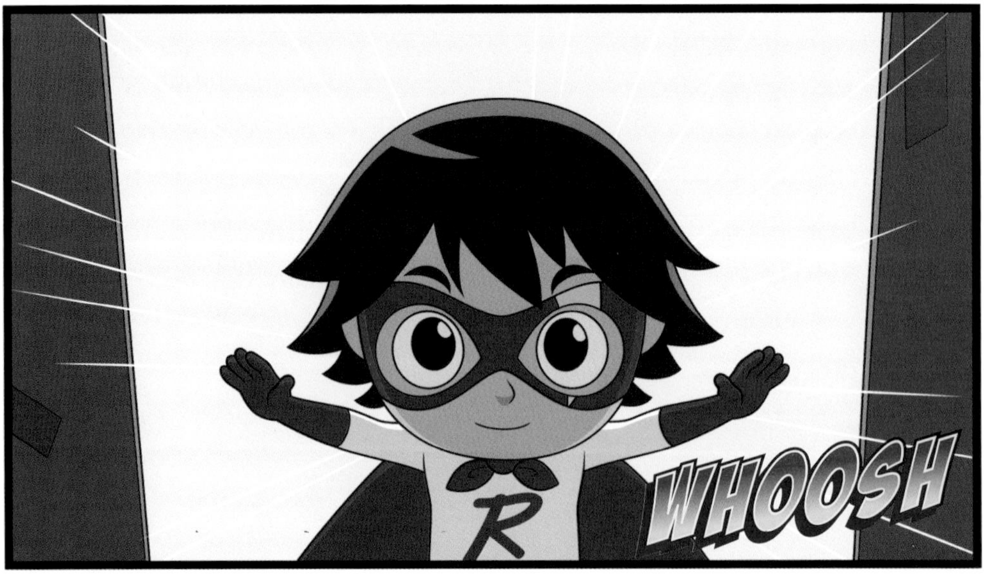
WHOOSH

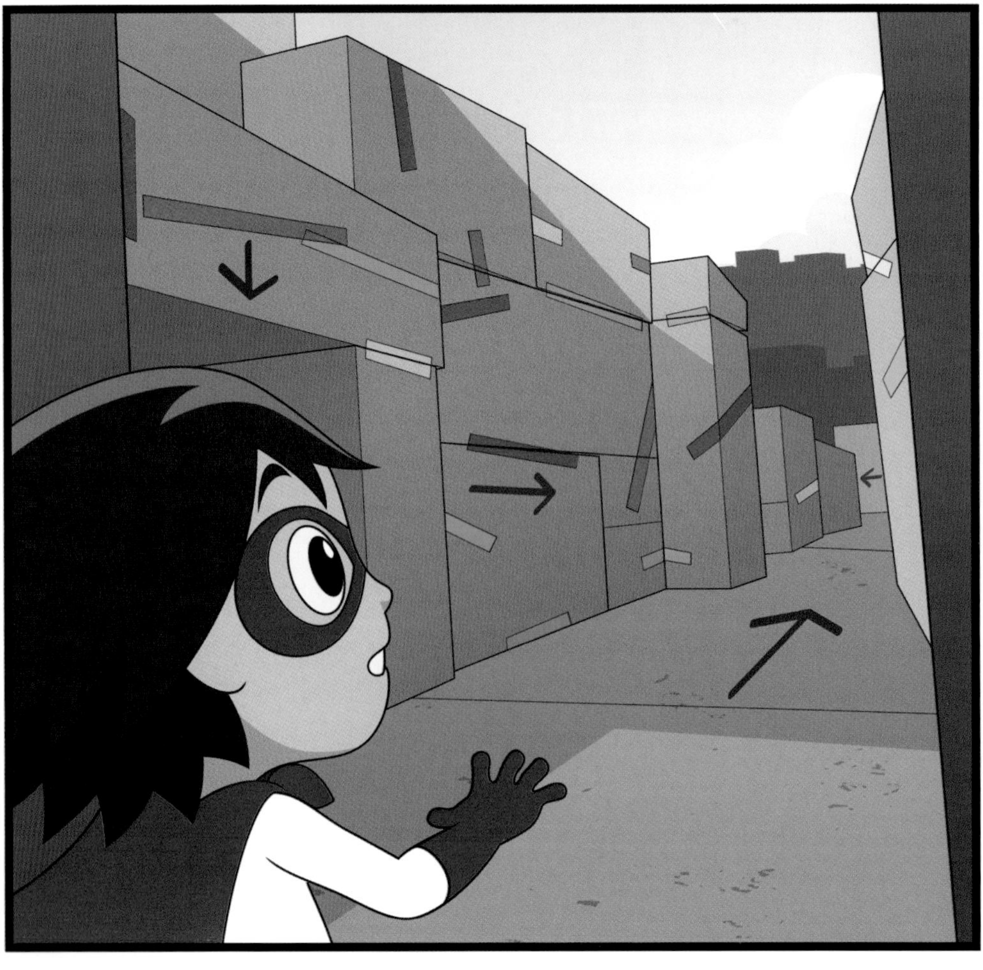

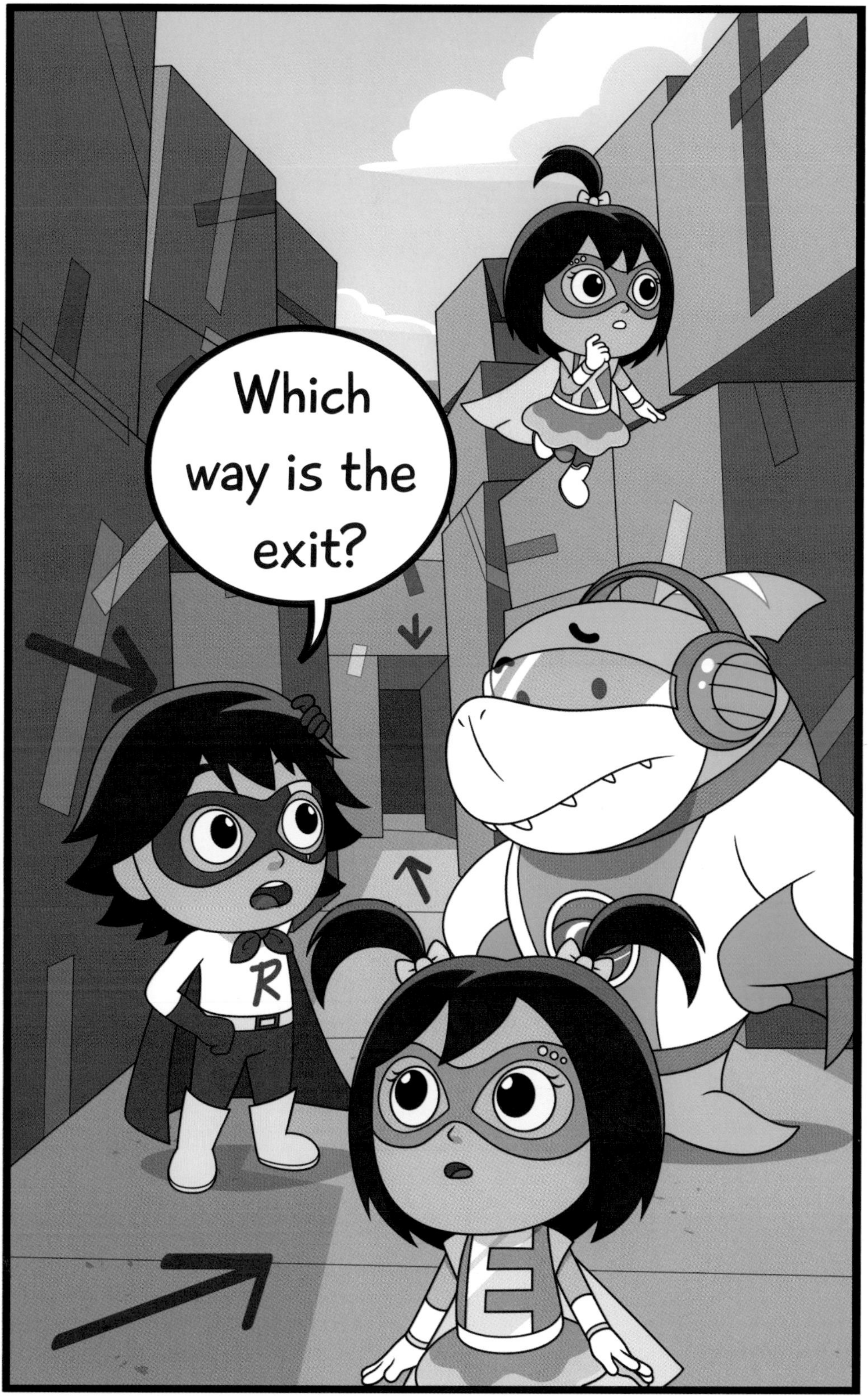
Which way is the exit?

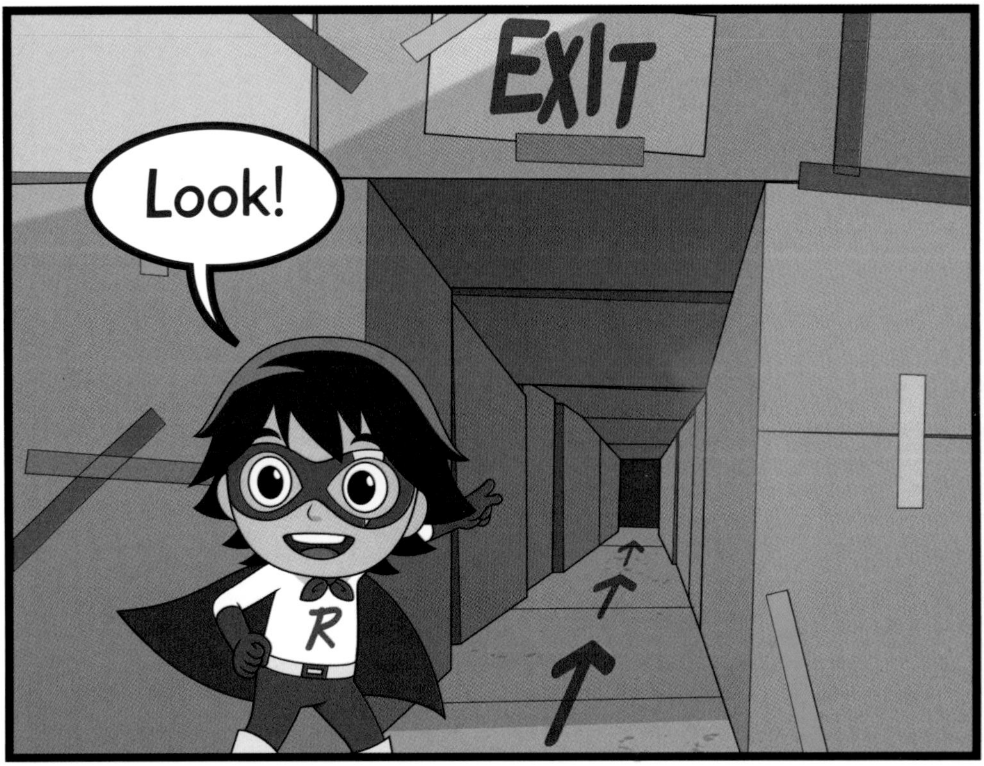
EXIT
Look!

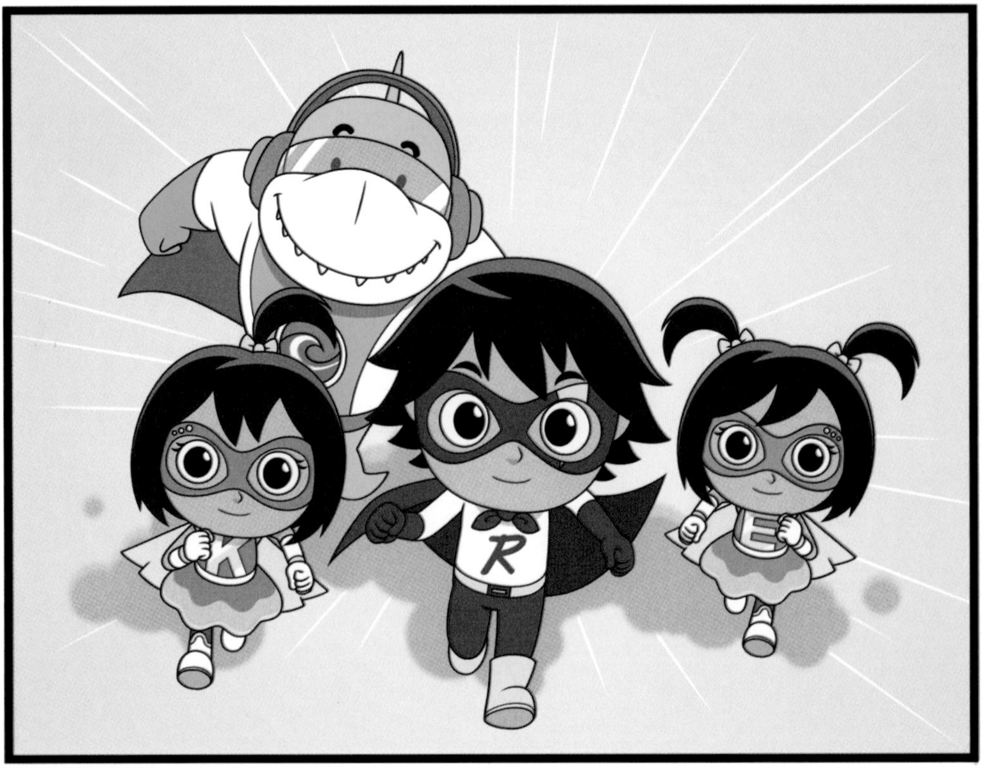

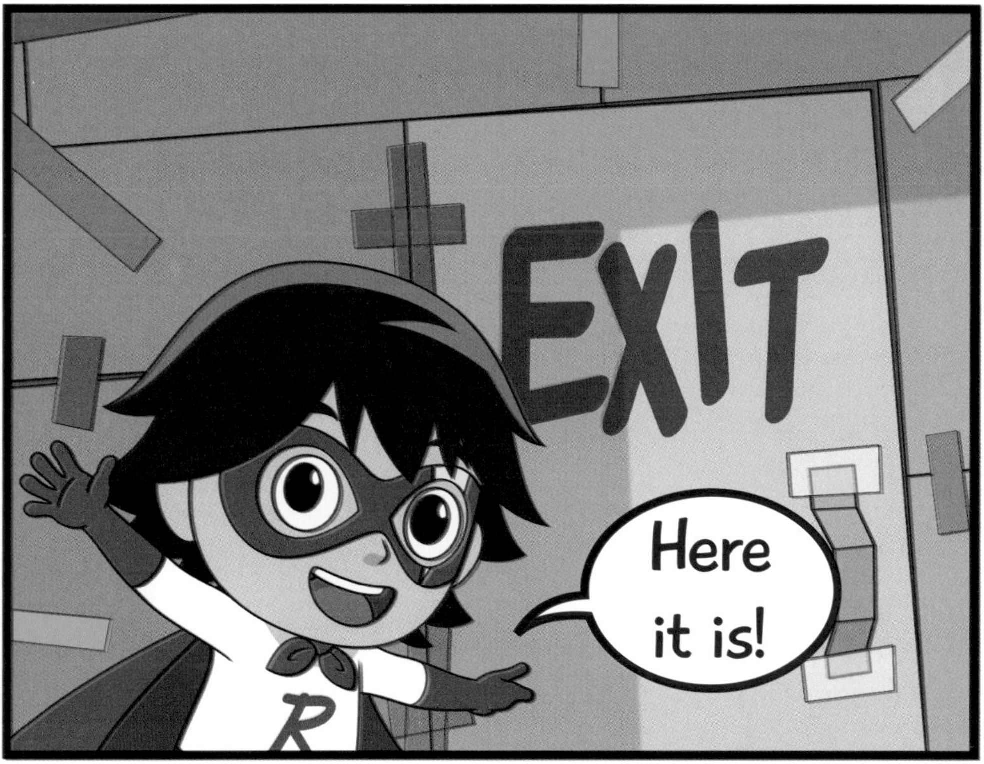
EXIT
Here it is!

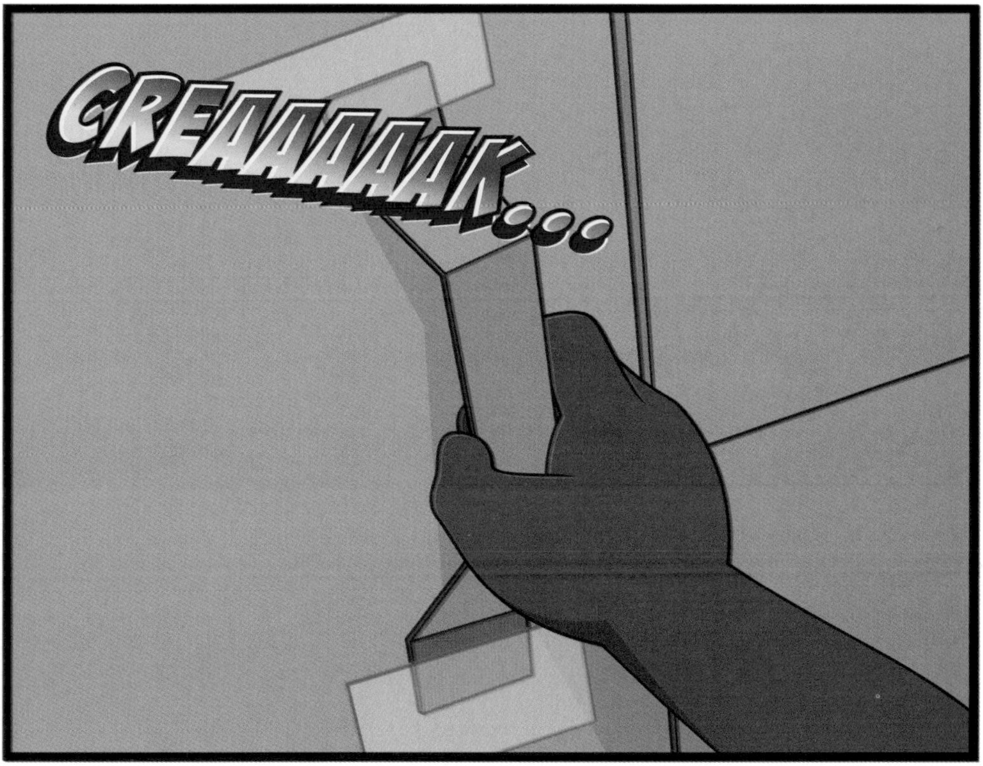
CREAAAAAAK...

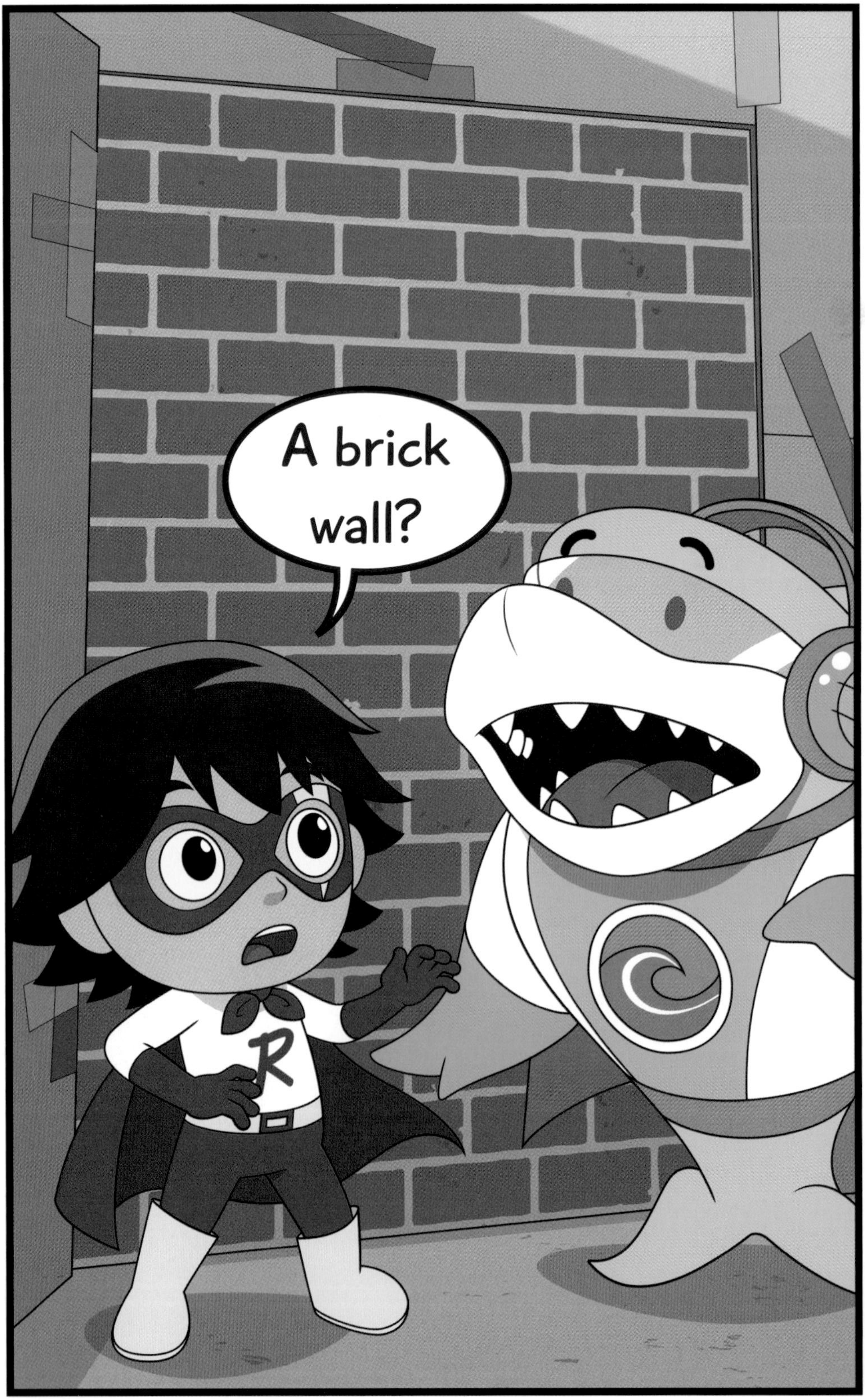
A brick wall?

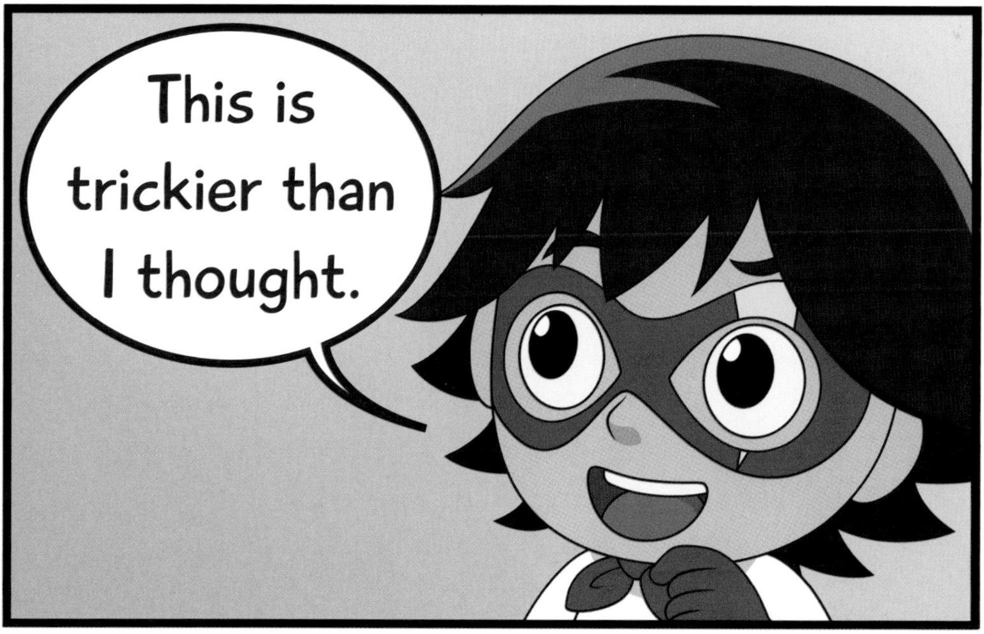
This is trickier than I thought.

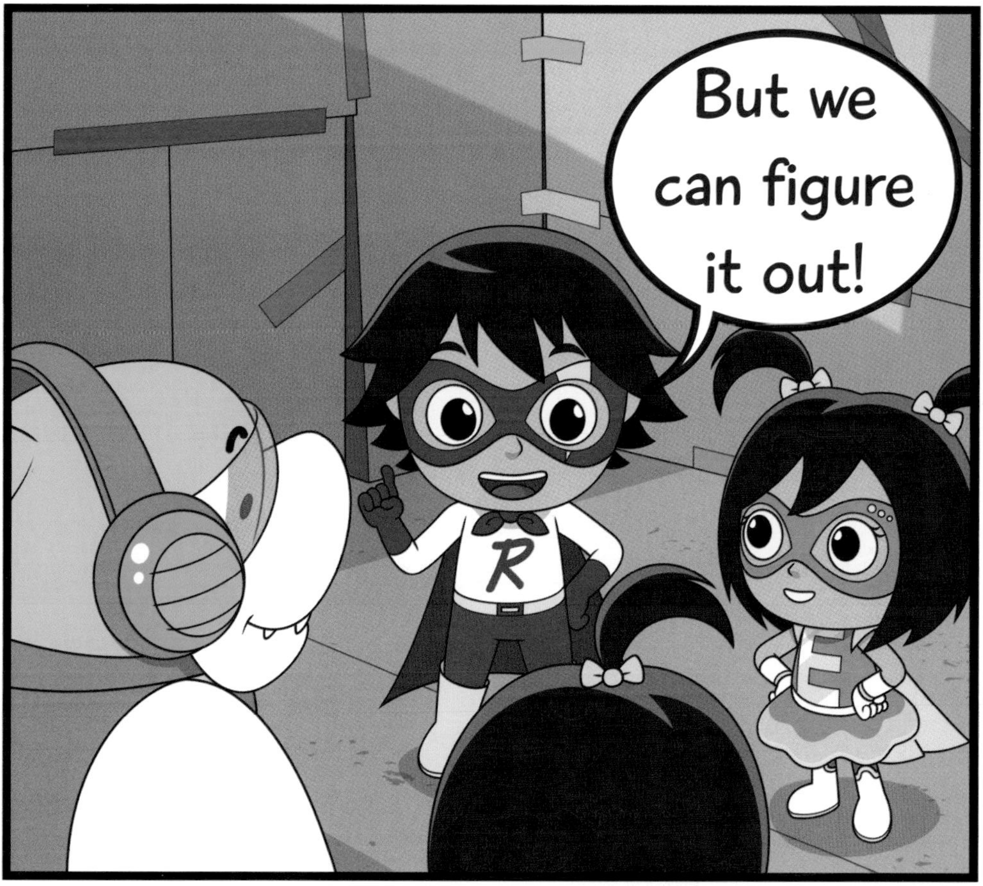
But we can figure it out!

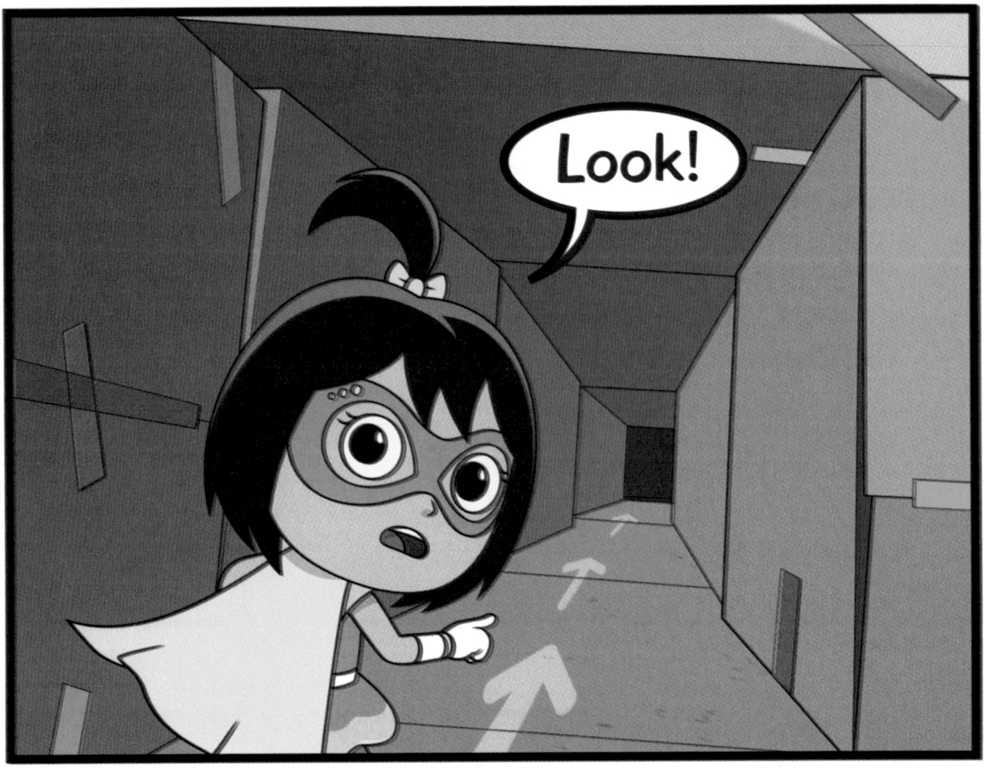
Look!

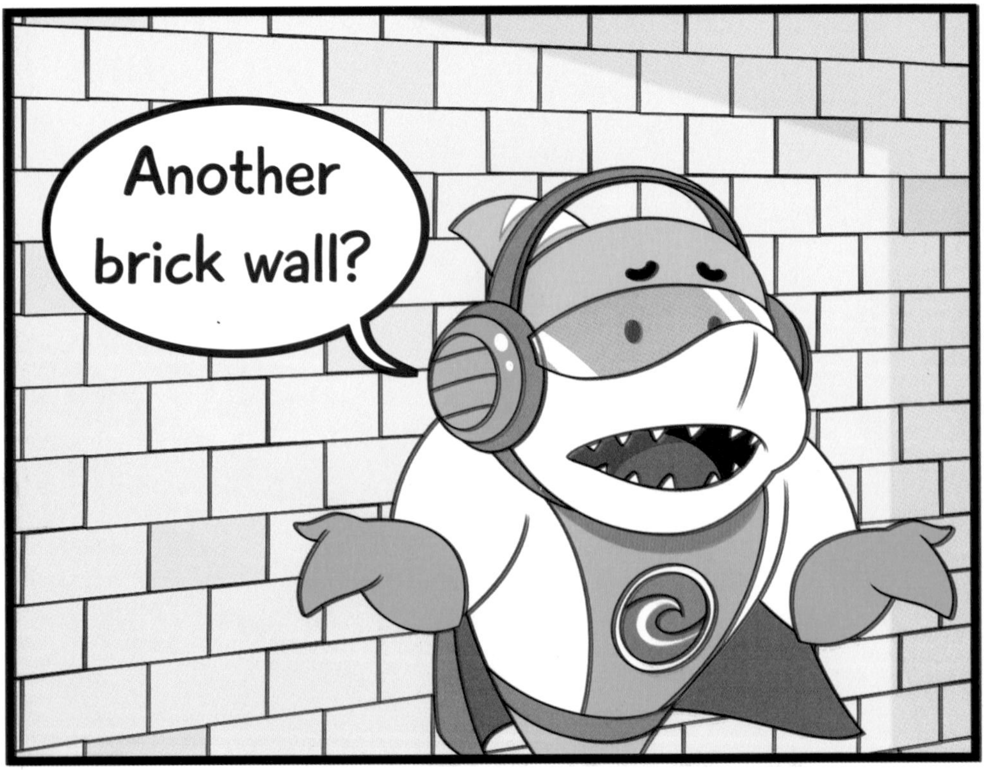
Another brick wall?

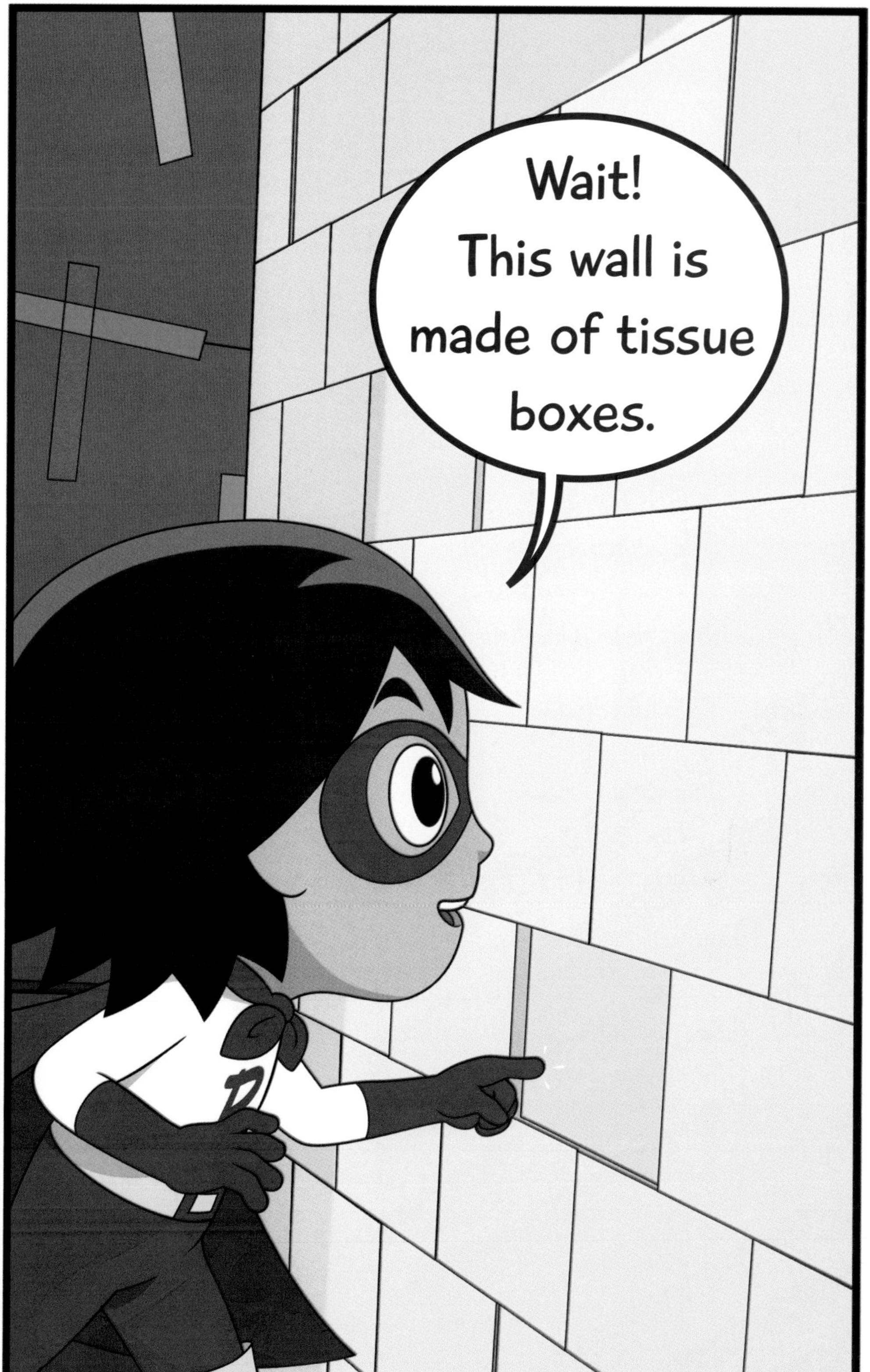
Wait!
This wall is made of tissue boxes.

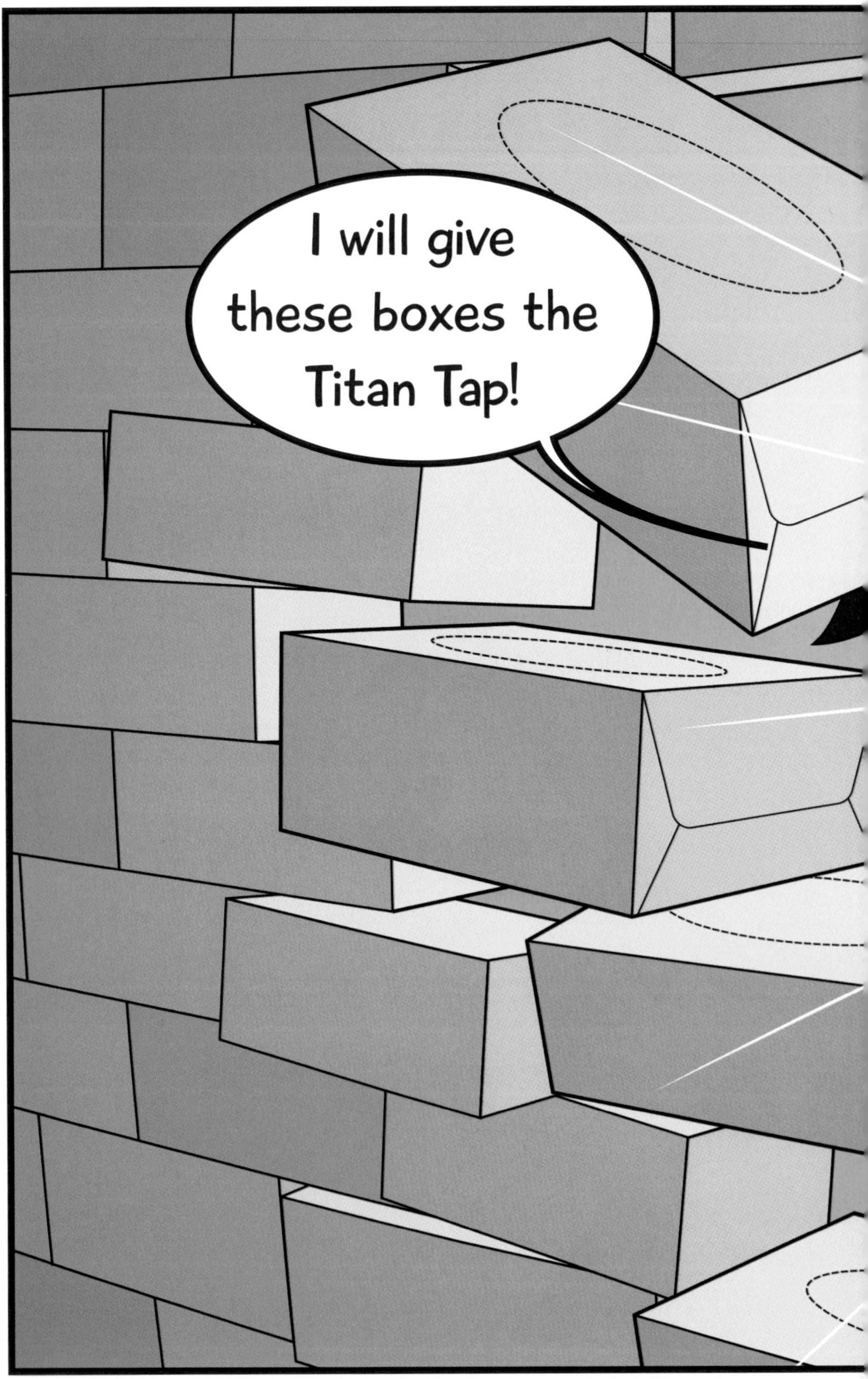
I will give these boxes the Titan Tap!

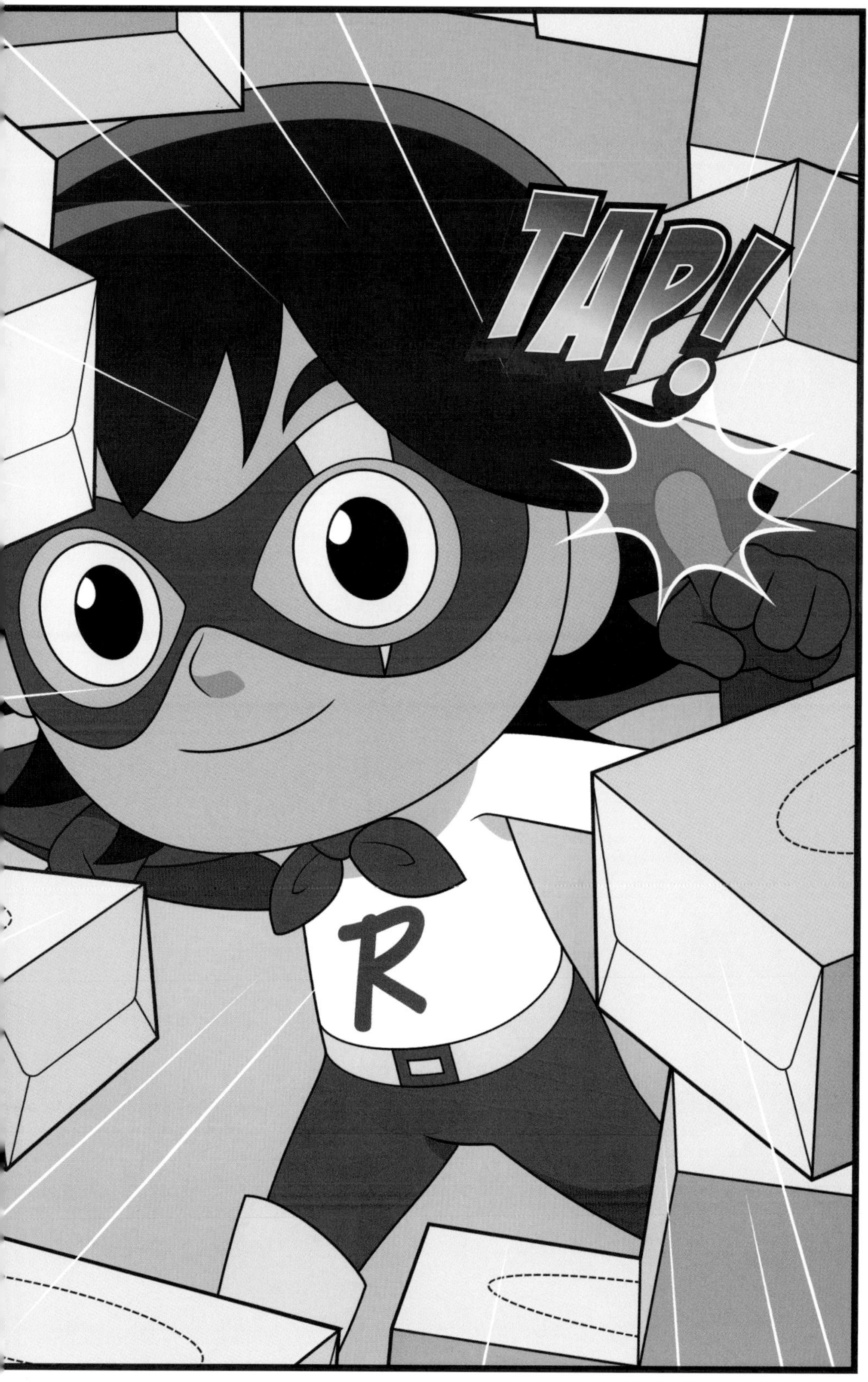
TAP!

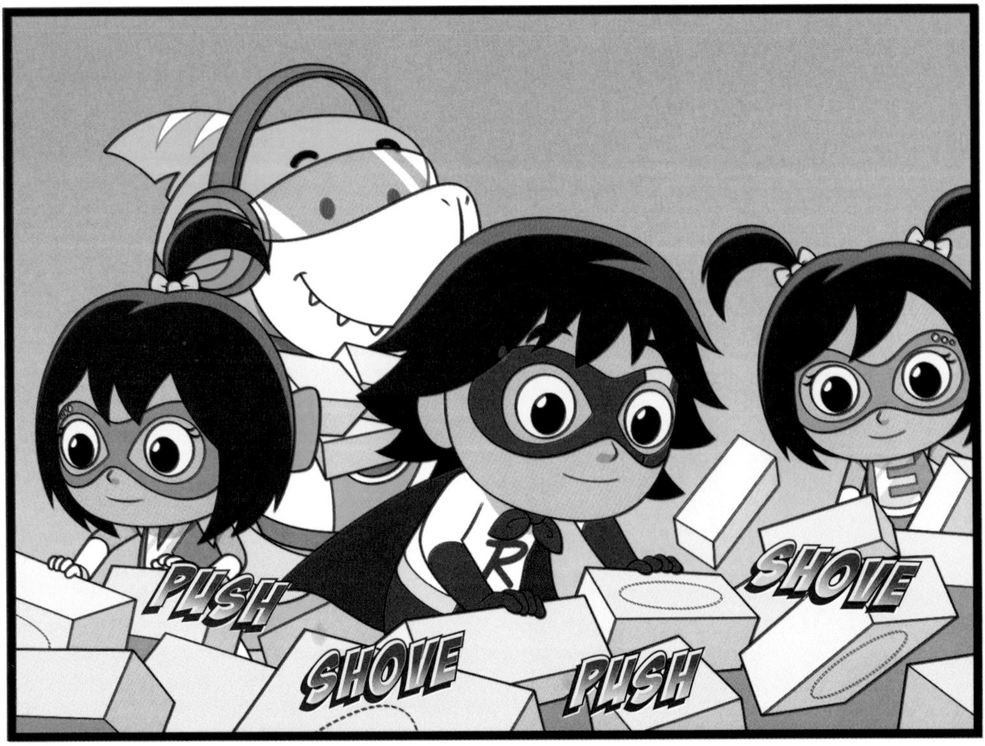
PUSH
SHOVE
PUSH
SHOVE

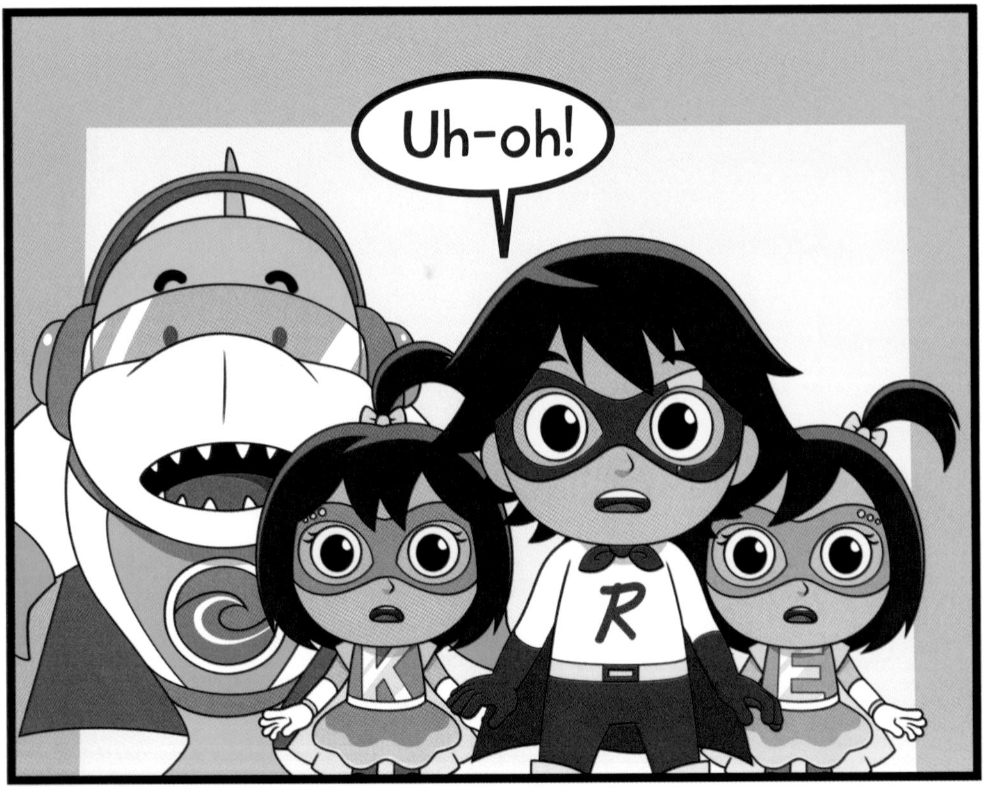
Uh-oh!

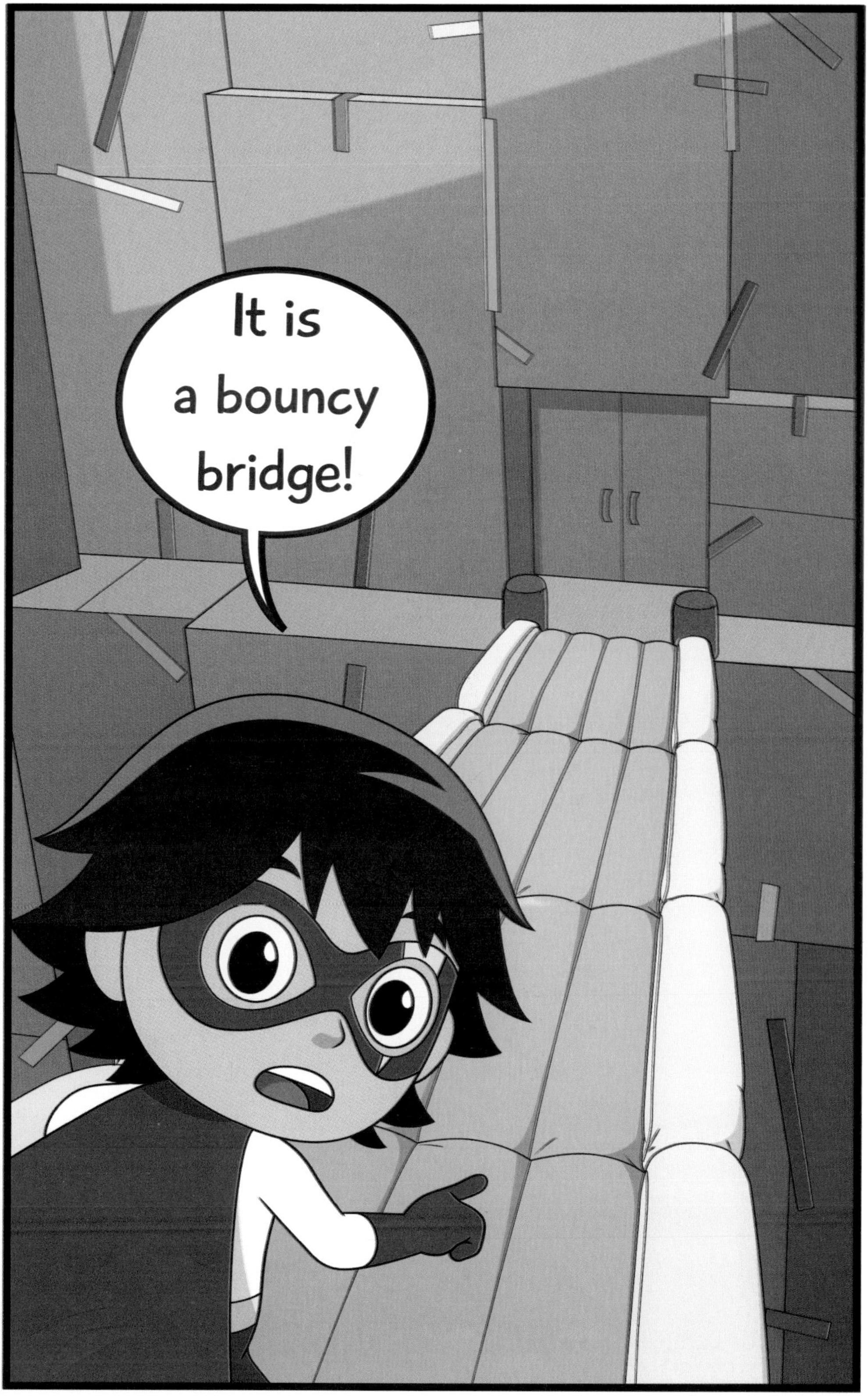
It is a bouncy bridge!

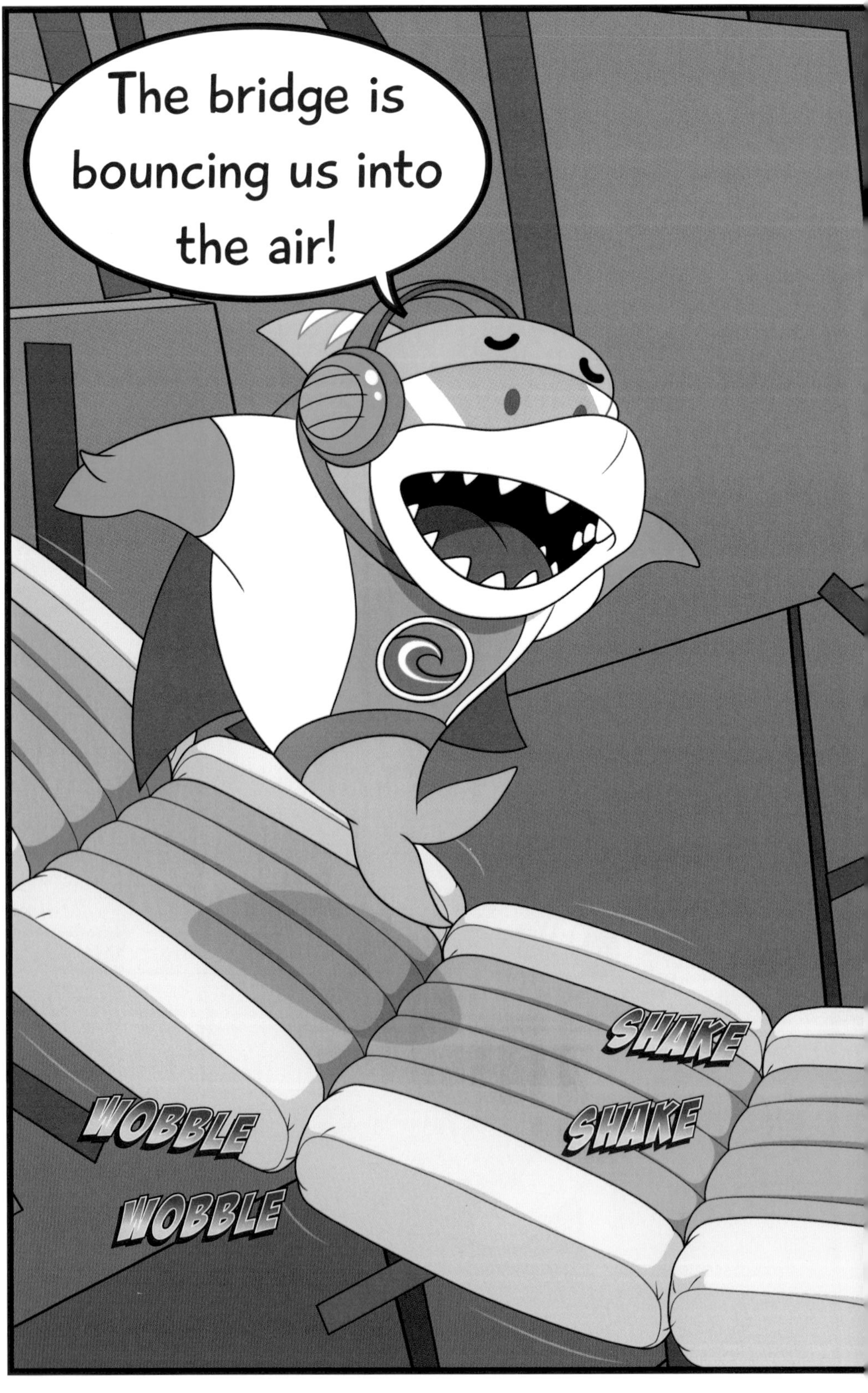
The bridge is bouncing us into the air!
SHAKE
SHAKE
WOBBLE
WOBBLE

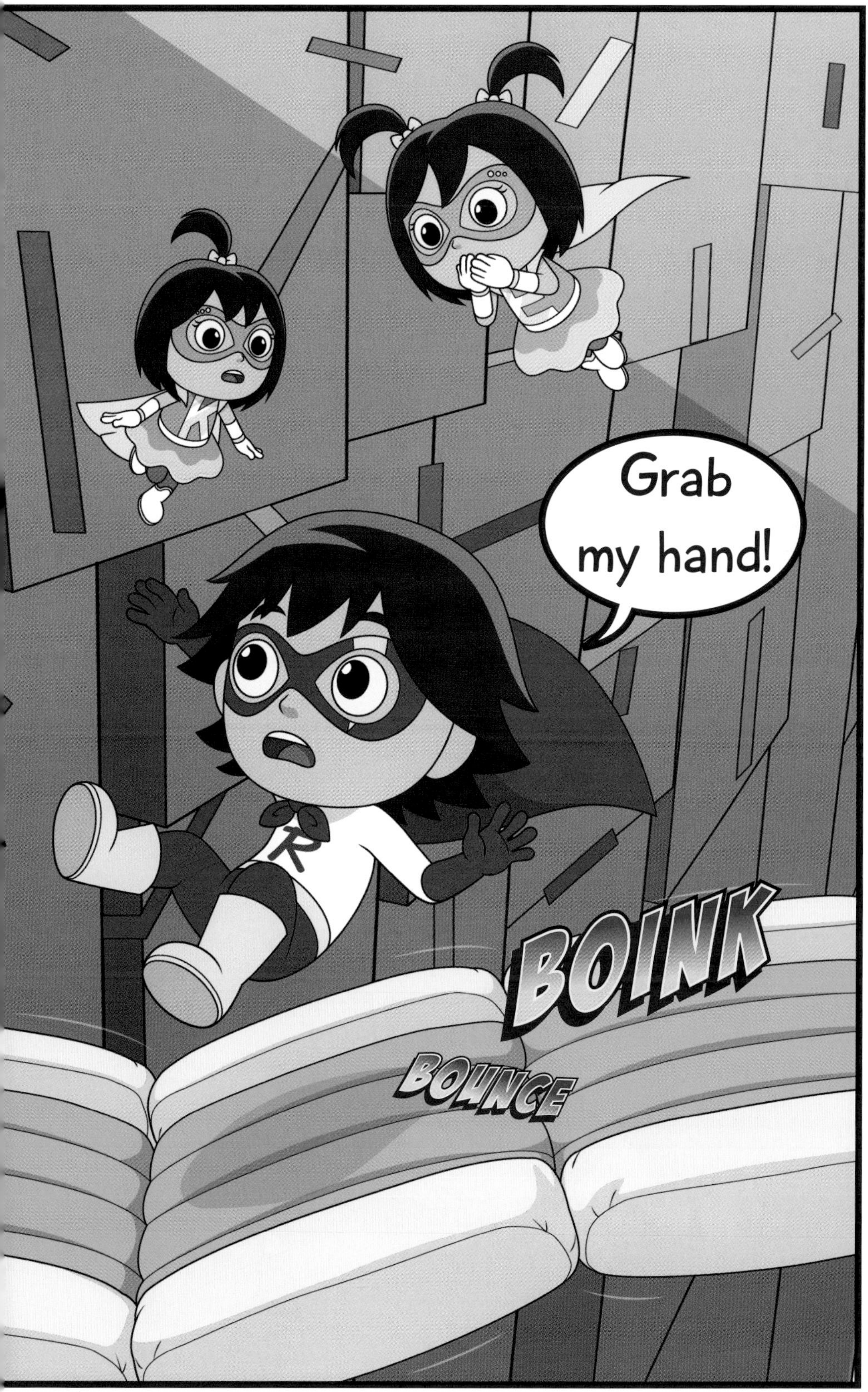
Grab my hand!
BOINK
BOUNCE

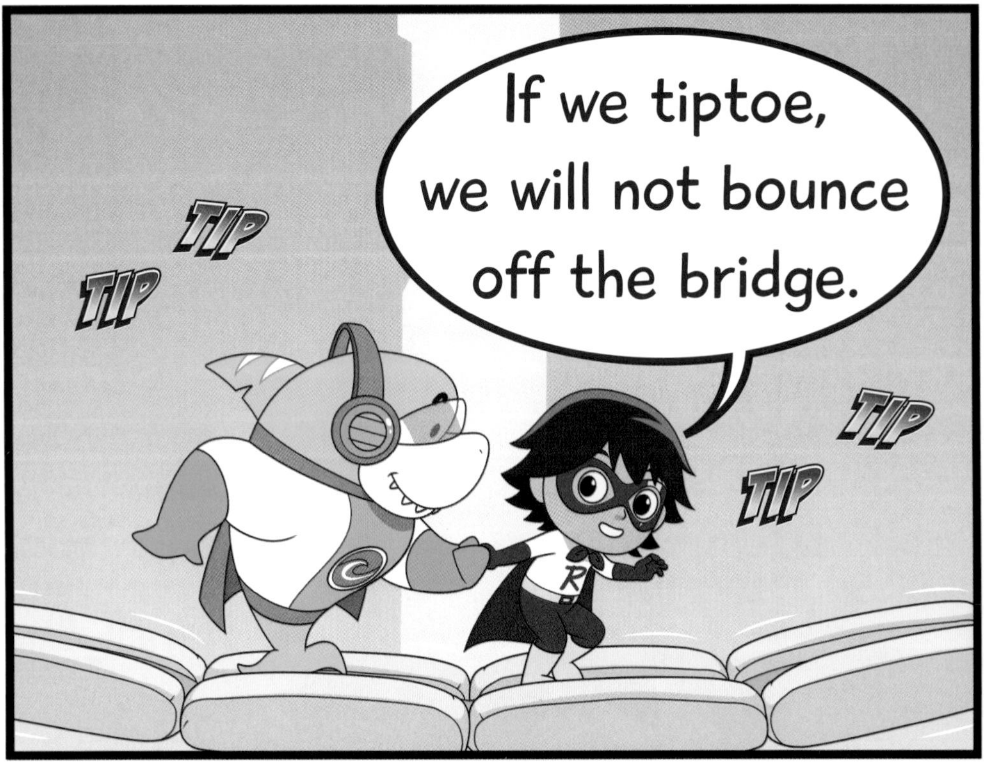
TIP
TIP
If we tiptoe, we will not bounce off the bridge.
TIP
TIP

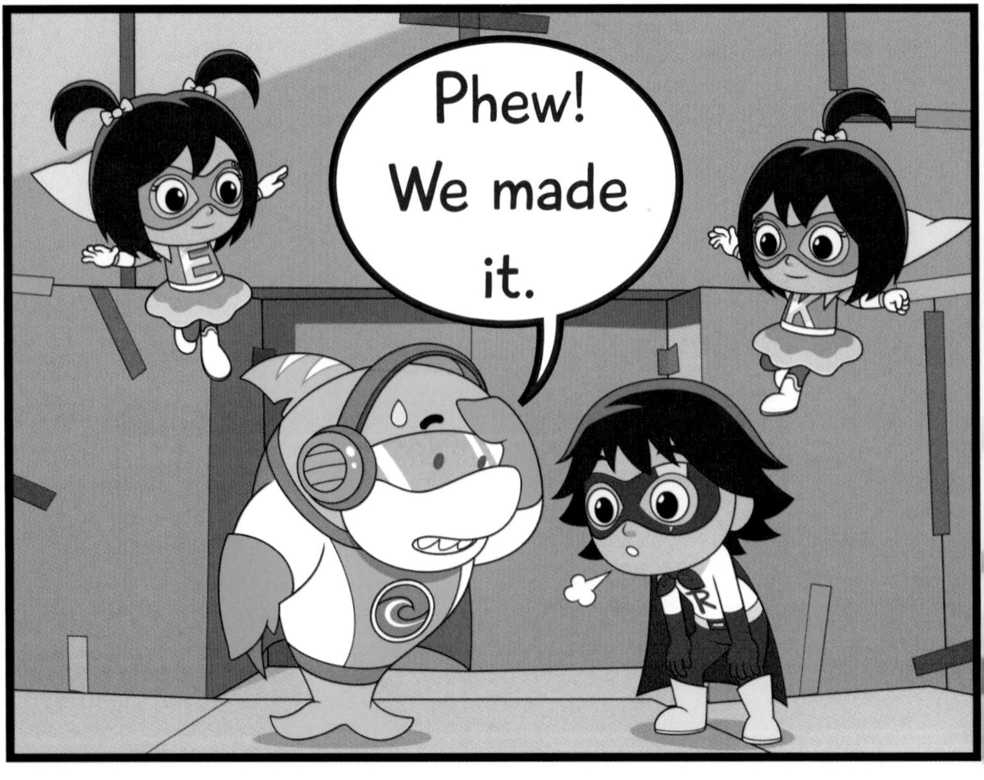
Phew! We made it.

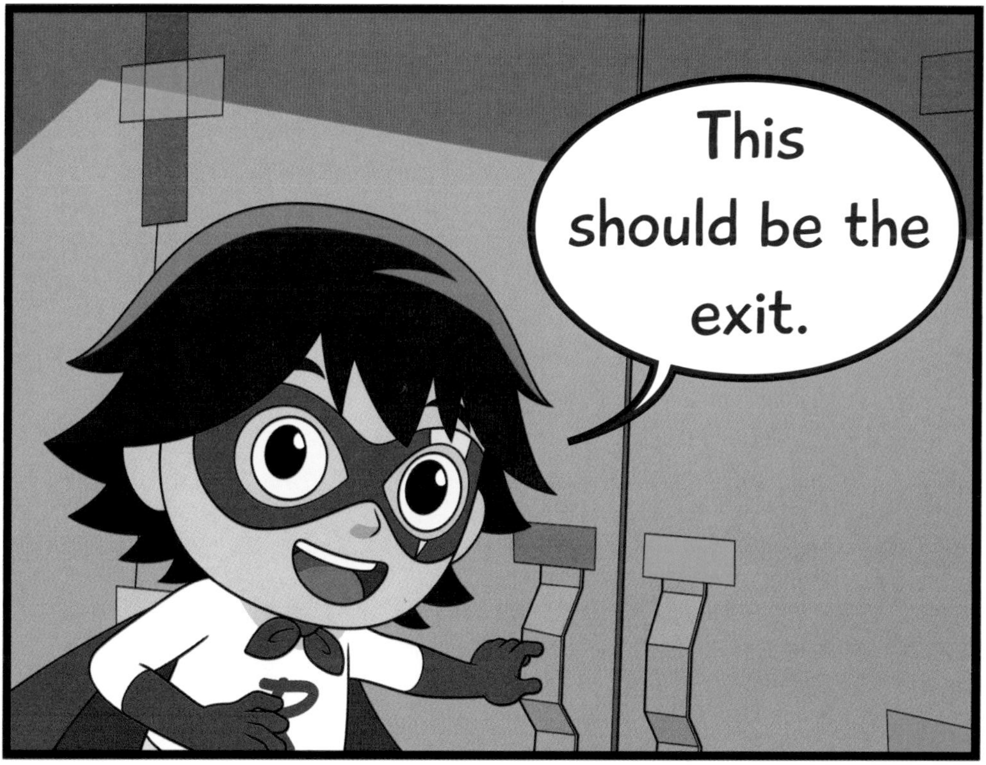
This should be the exit.

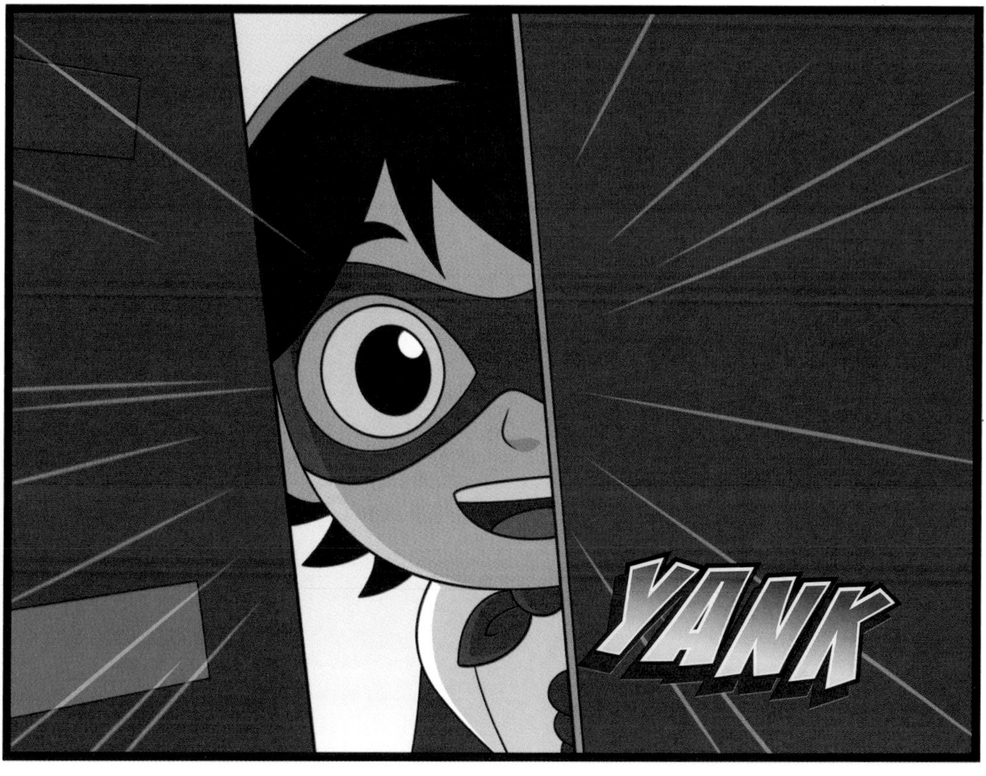
YANK

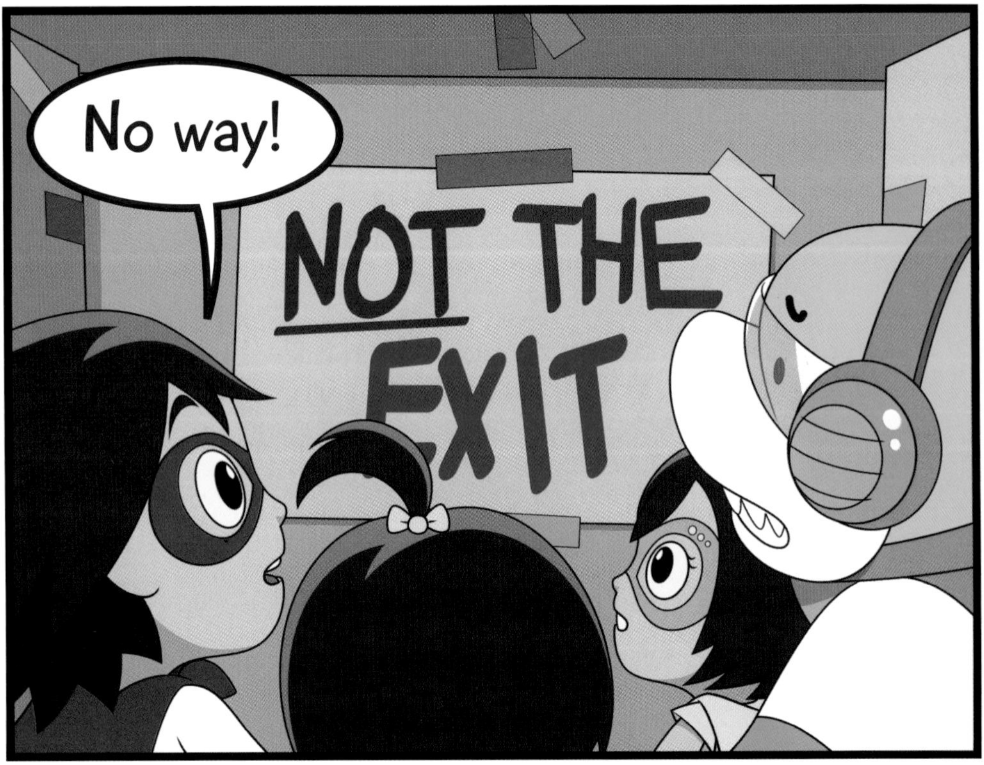
No way!
NOT THE EXIT

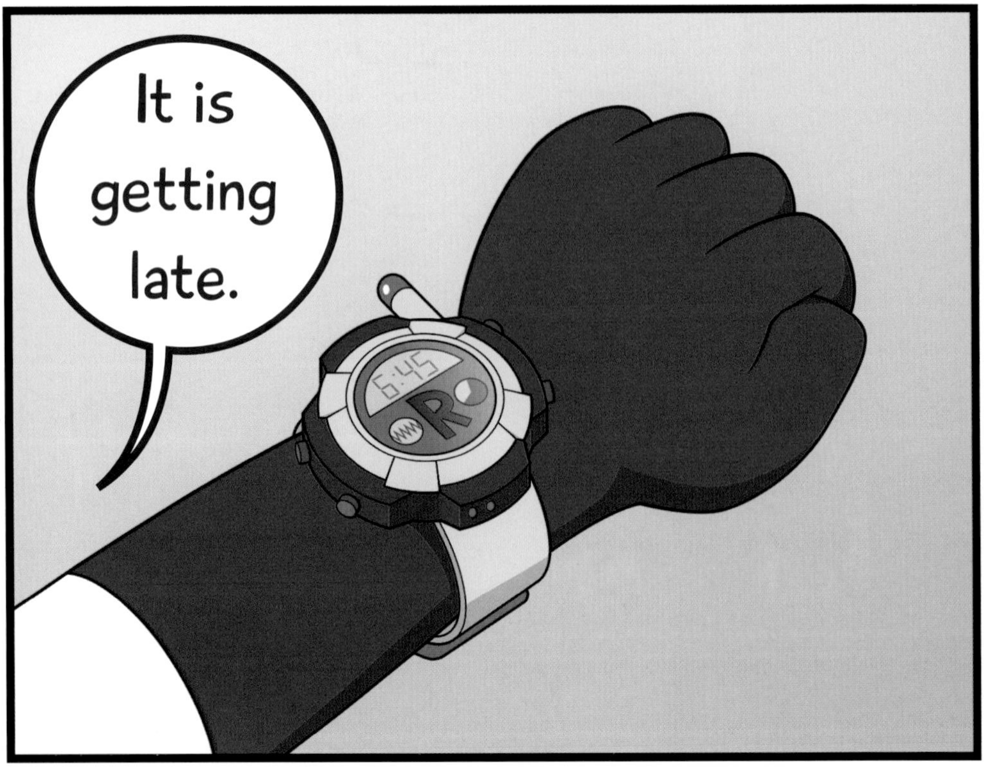
It is getting late.
6:45

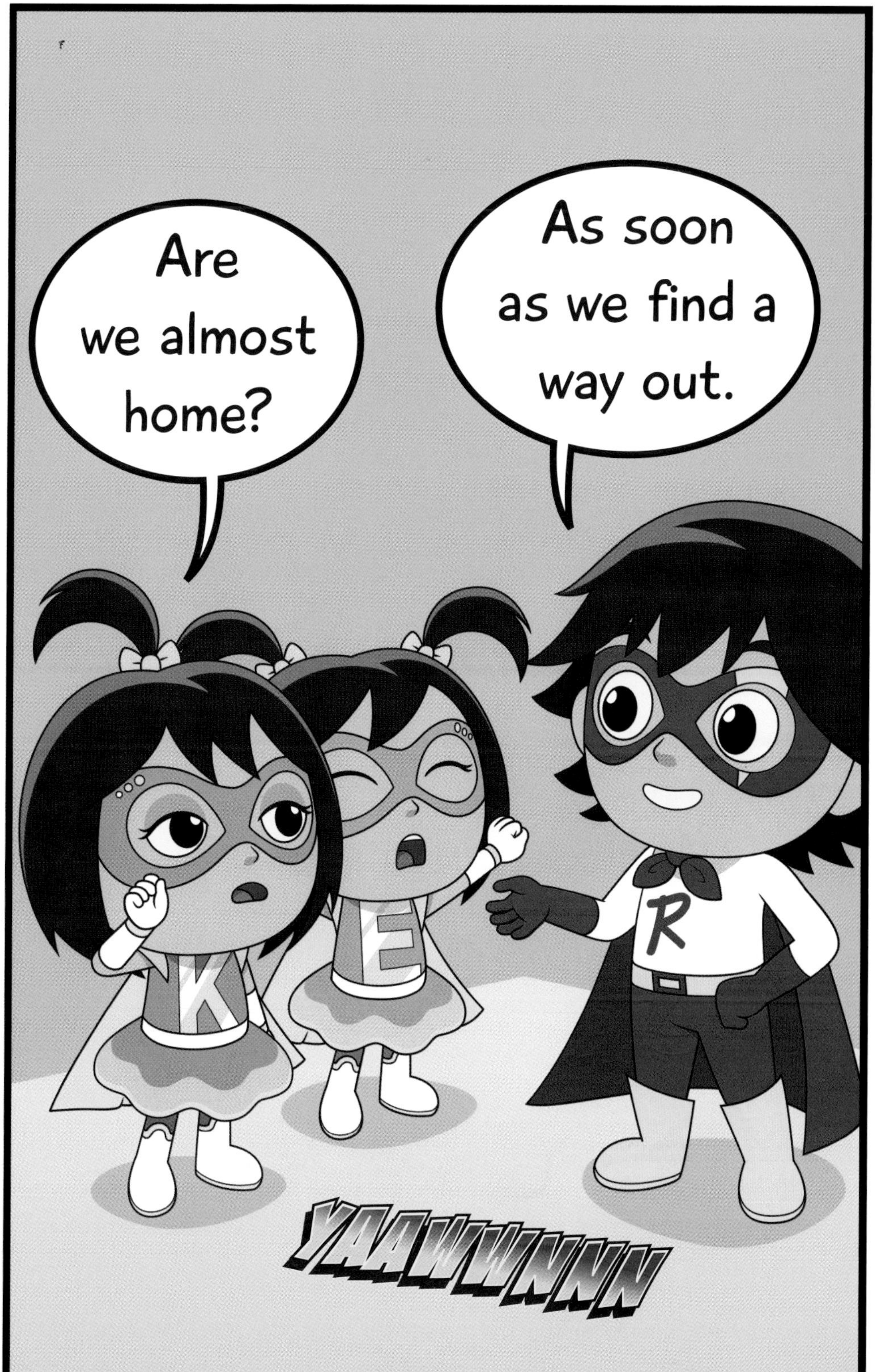
Are we almost home?
As soon as we find a way out.
YAAWWNNN

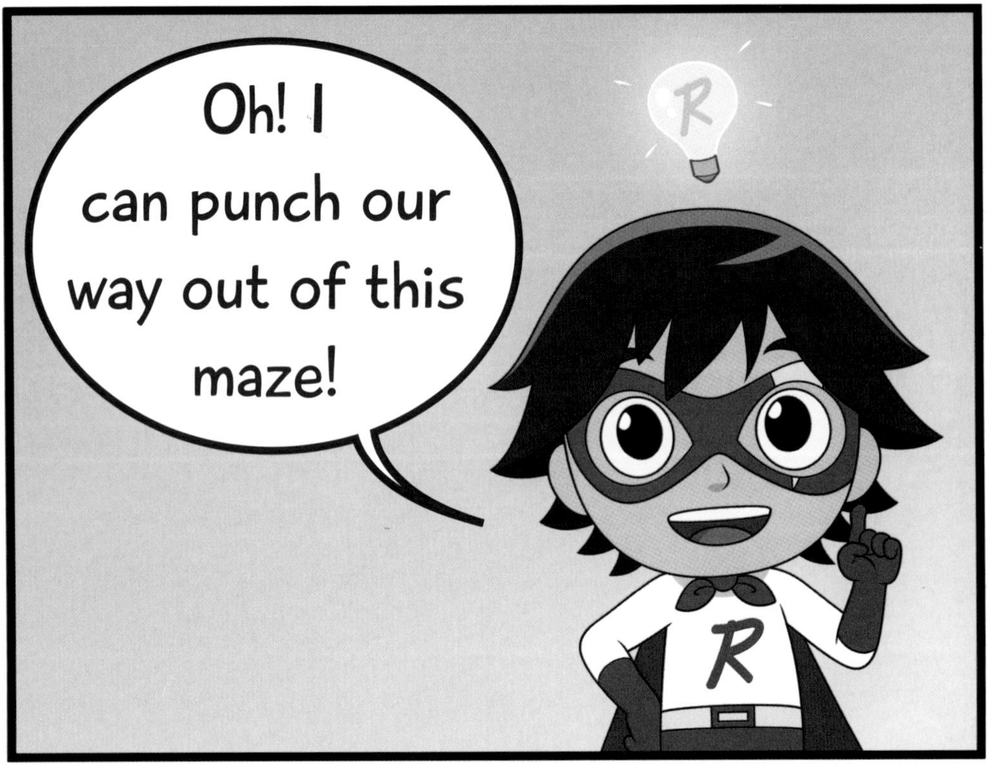
Oh! I can punch our way out of this maze!

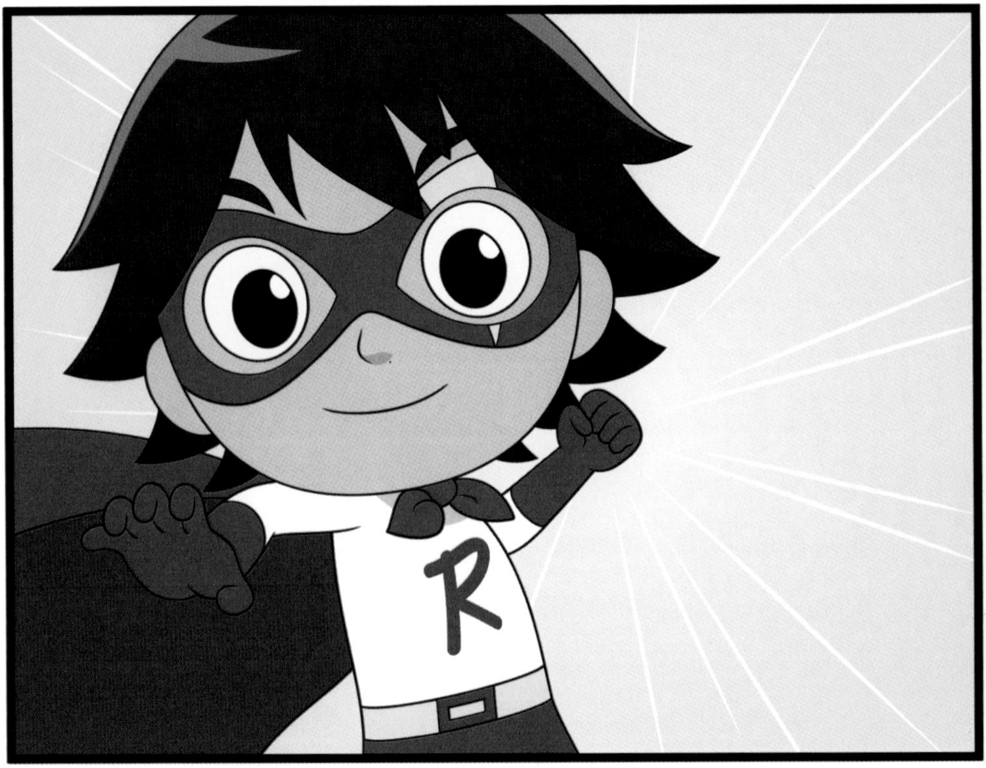

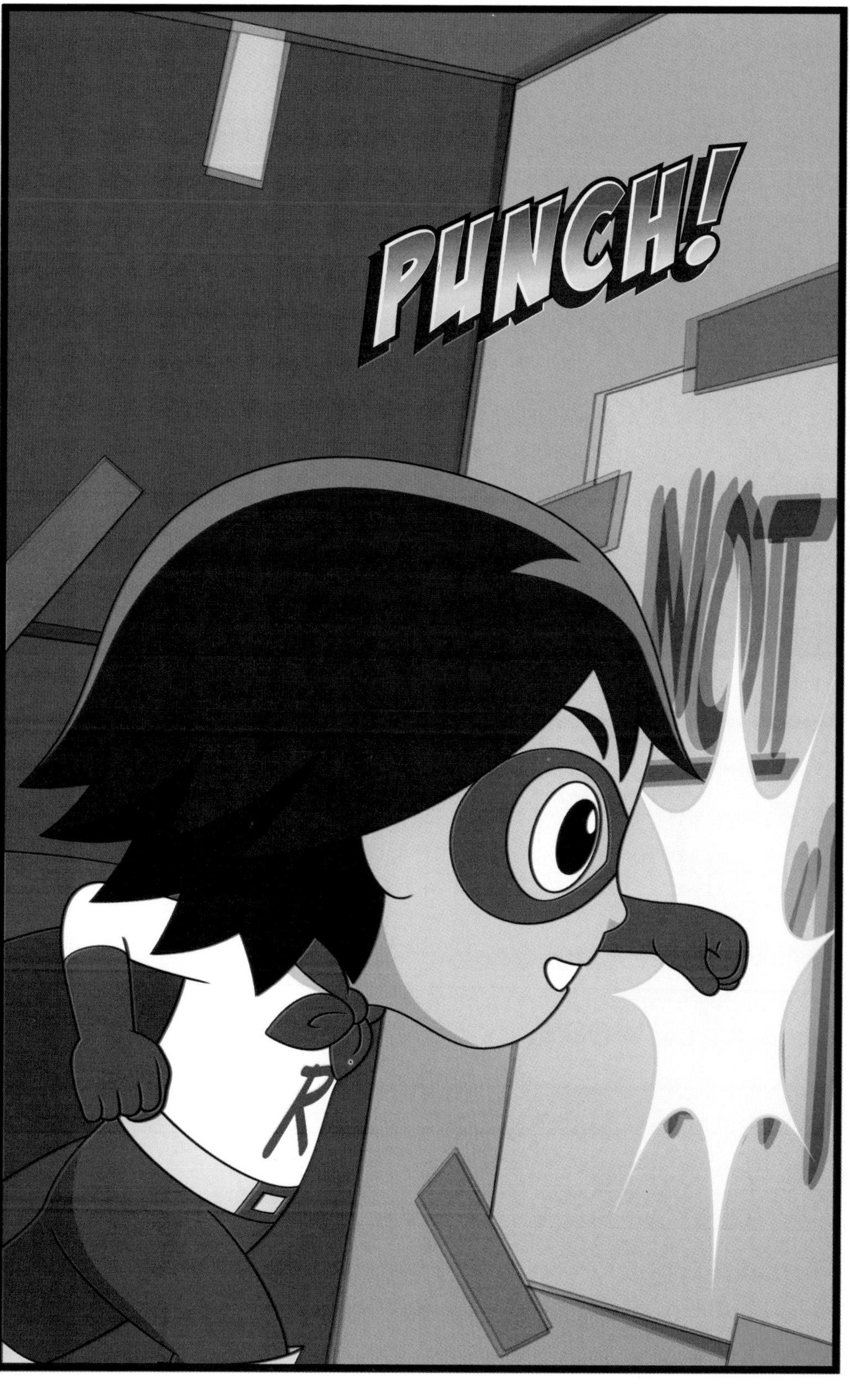
PUNCH!
NOT

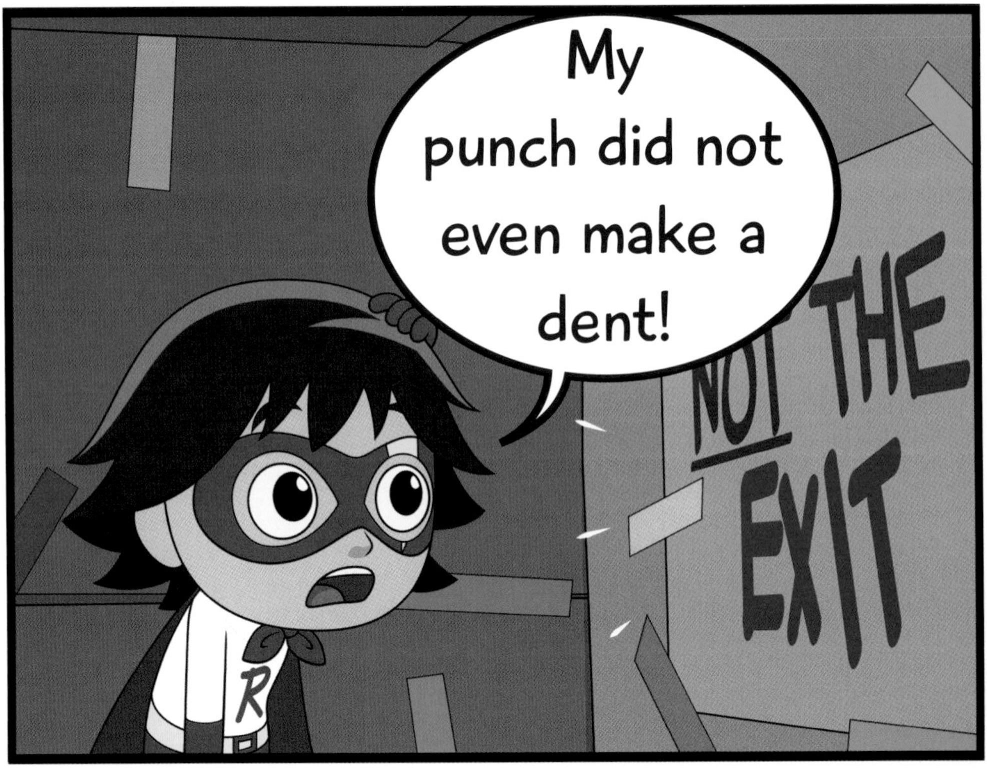
My punch did not even make a dent!
NOT THE EXIT

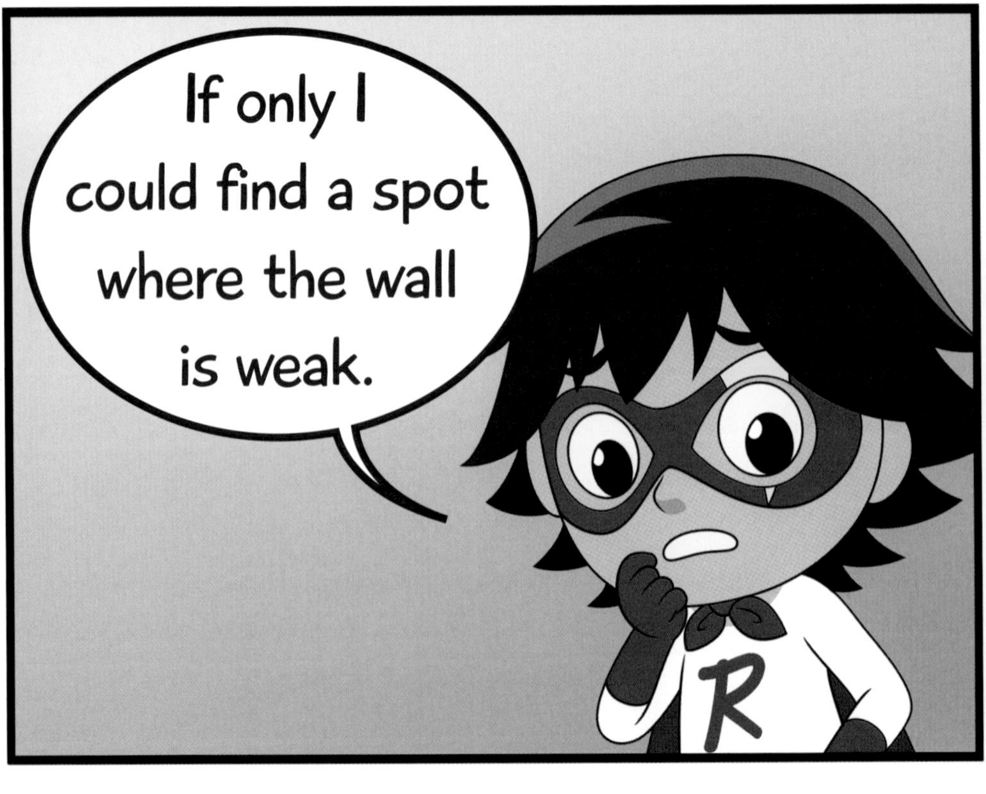
If only I could find a spot where the wall is weak.

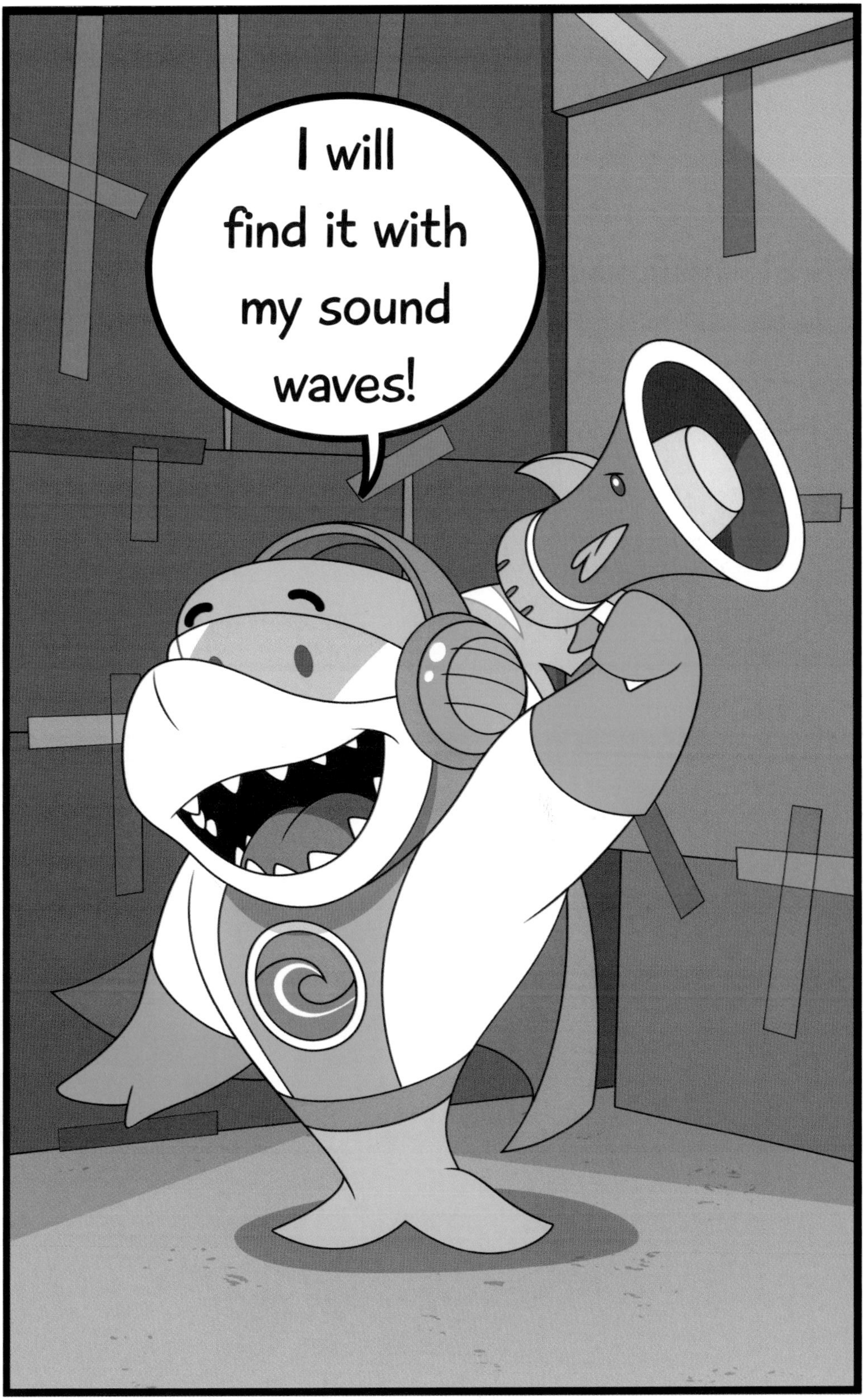
I will find it with my sound waves!

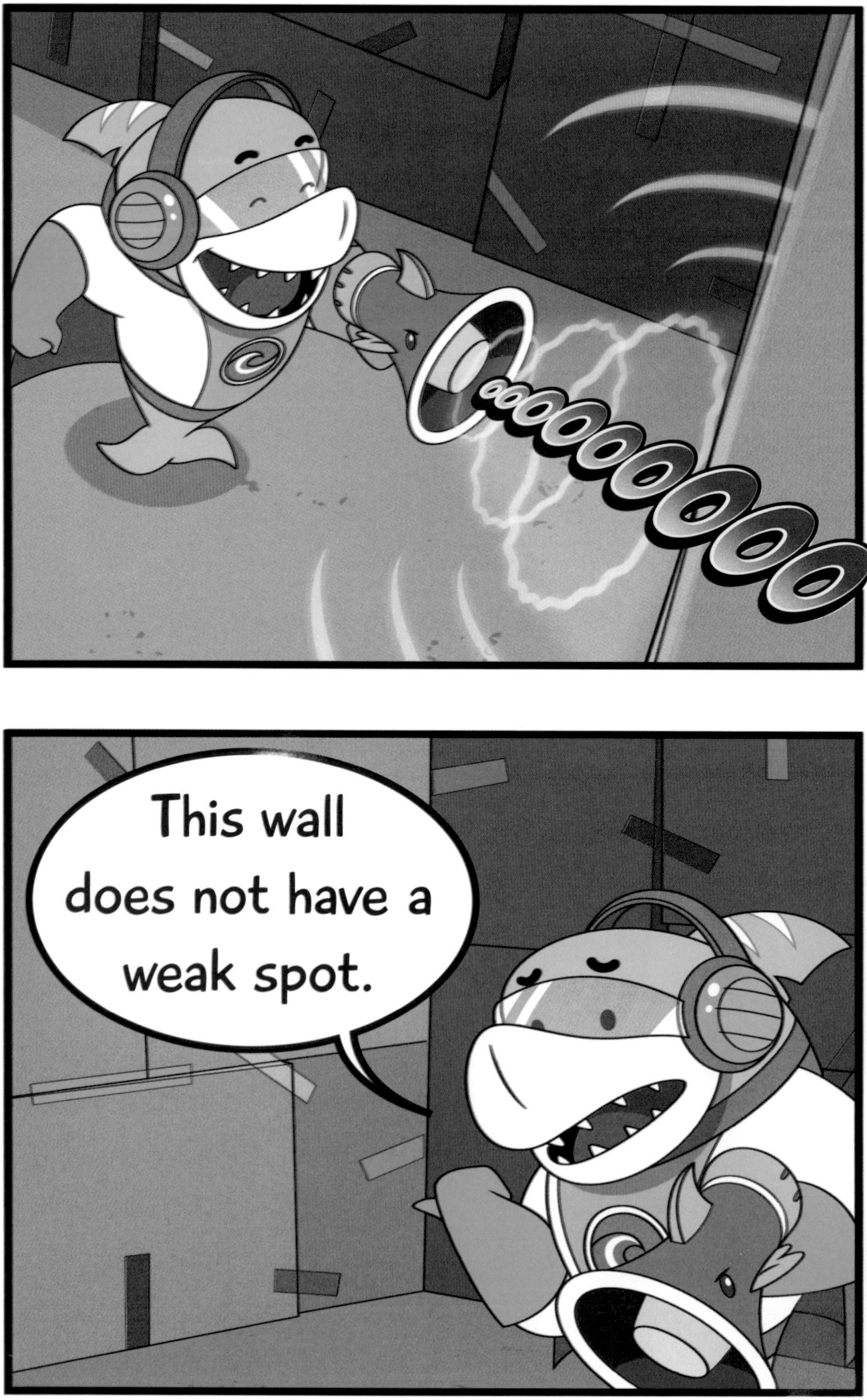
This wall does not have a weak spot.

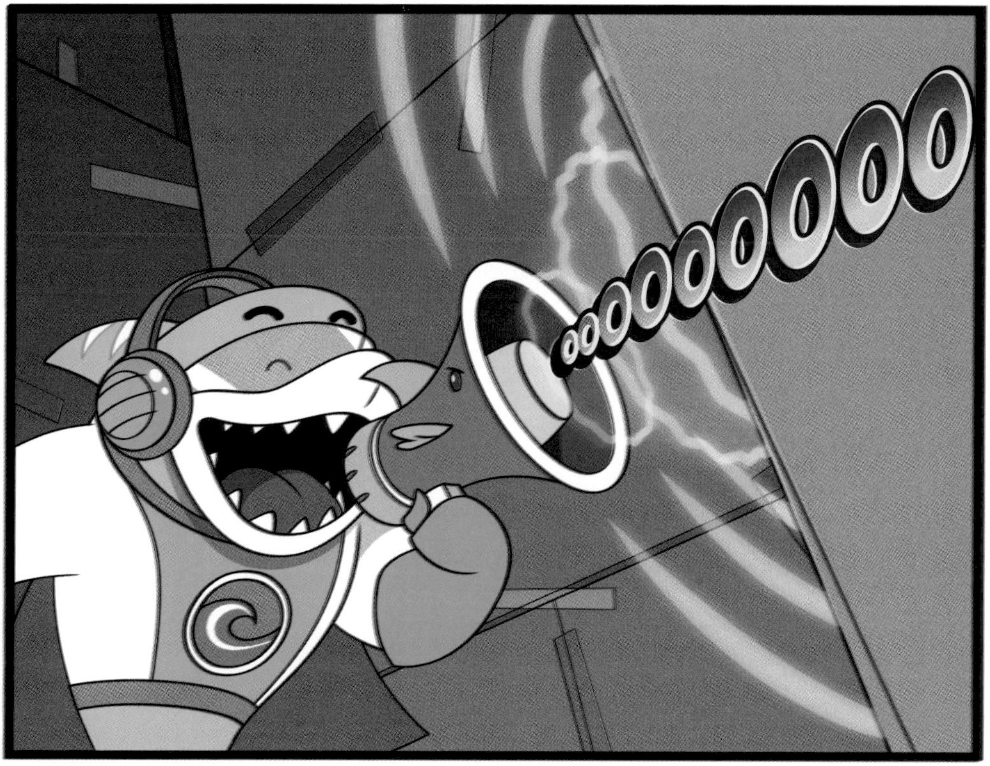
ooOOOOOOO

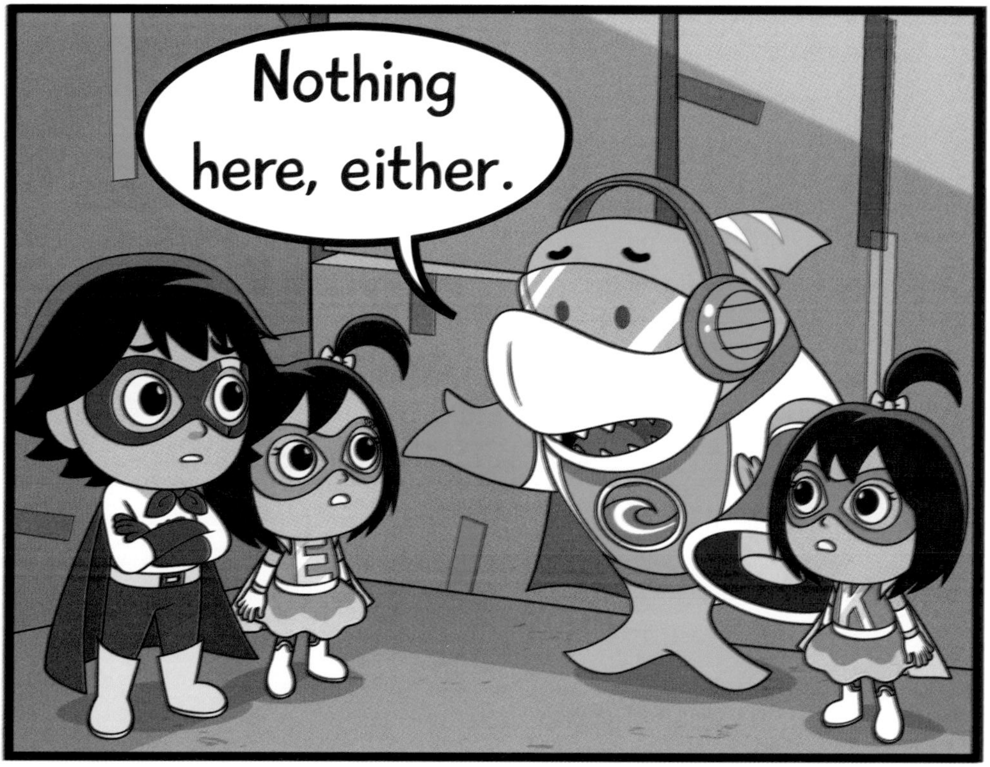
Nothing here, either.

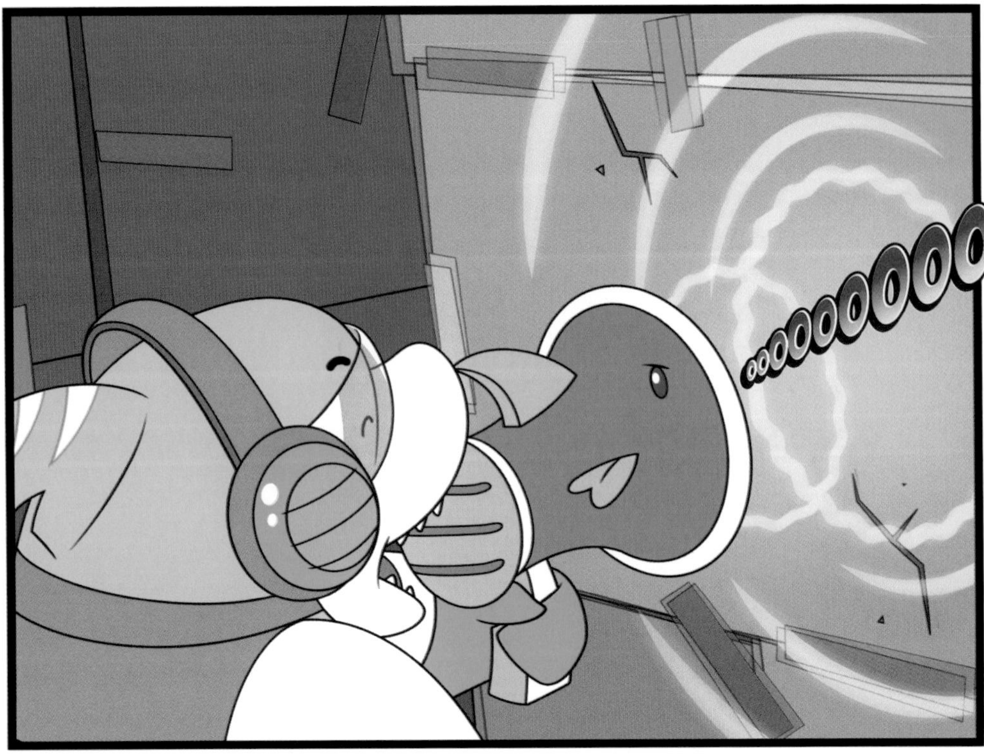
oooooOOOO

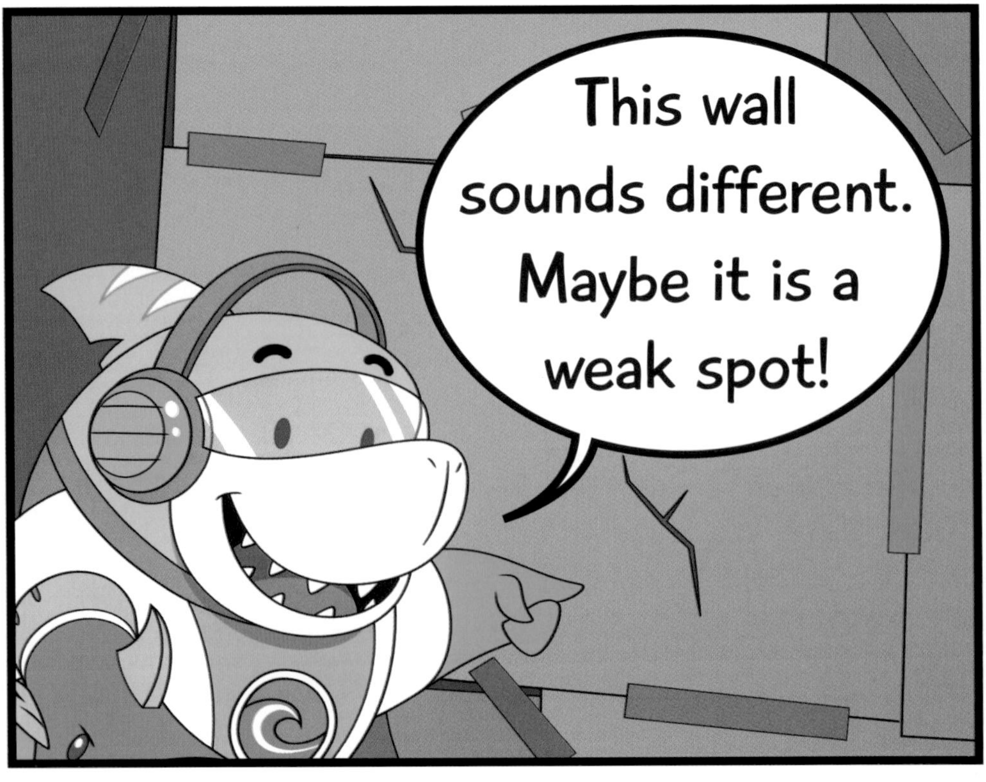
This wall sounds different. Maybe it is a weak spot!

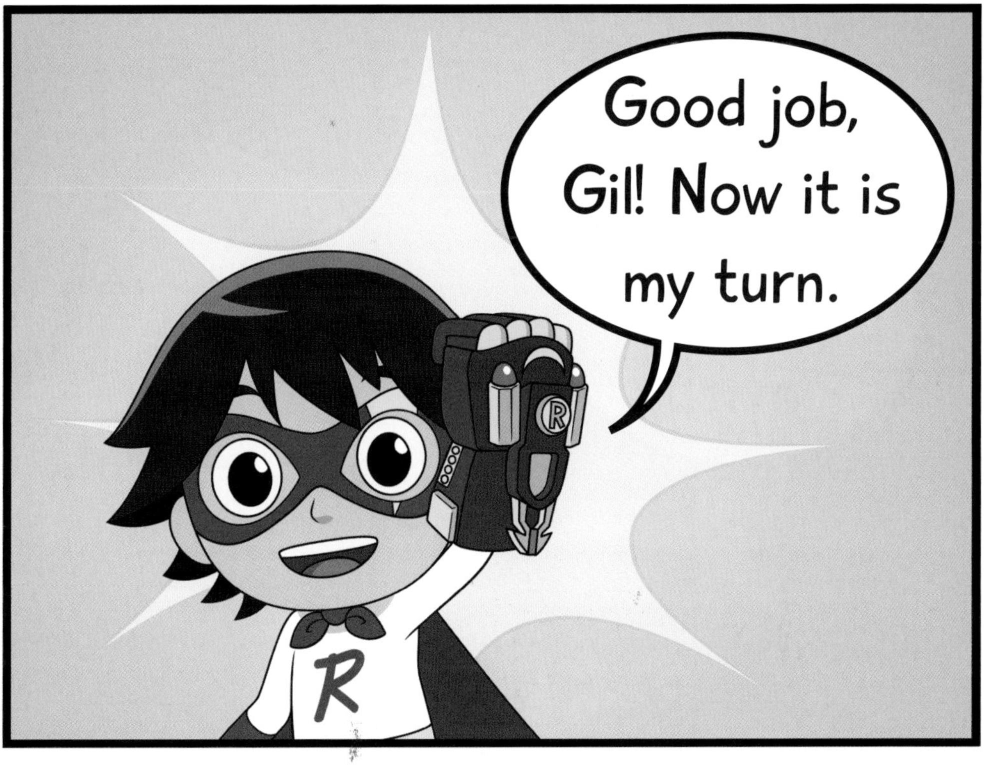
Good job, Gil! Now it is my turn.

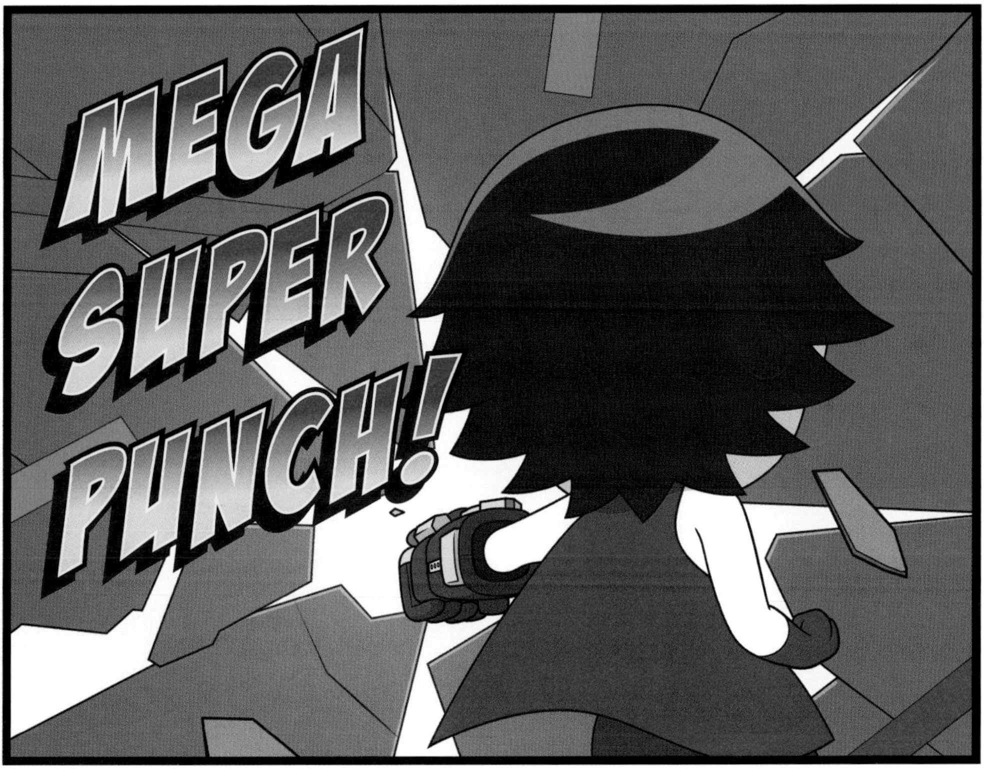
MEGA SUPER PUNCH!

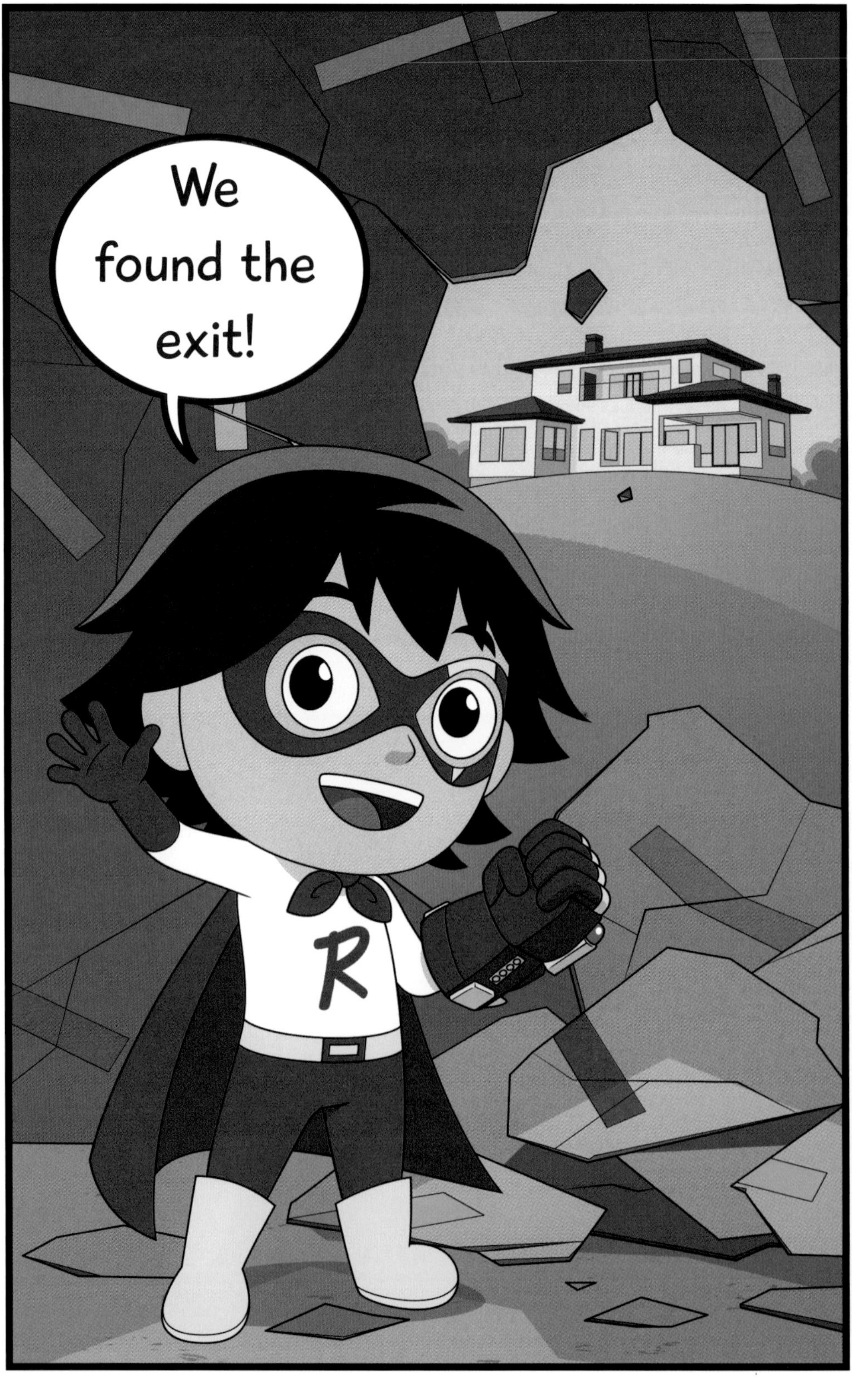
We found the exit!

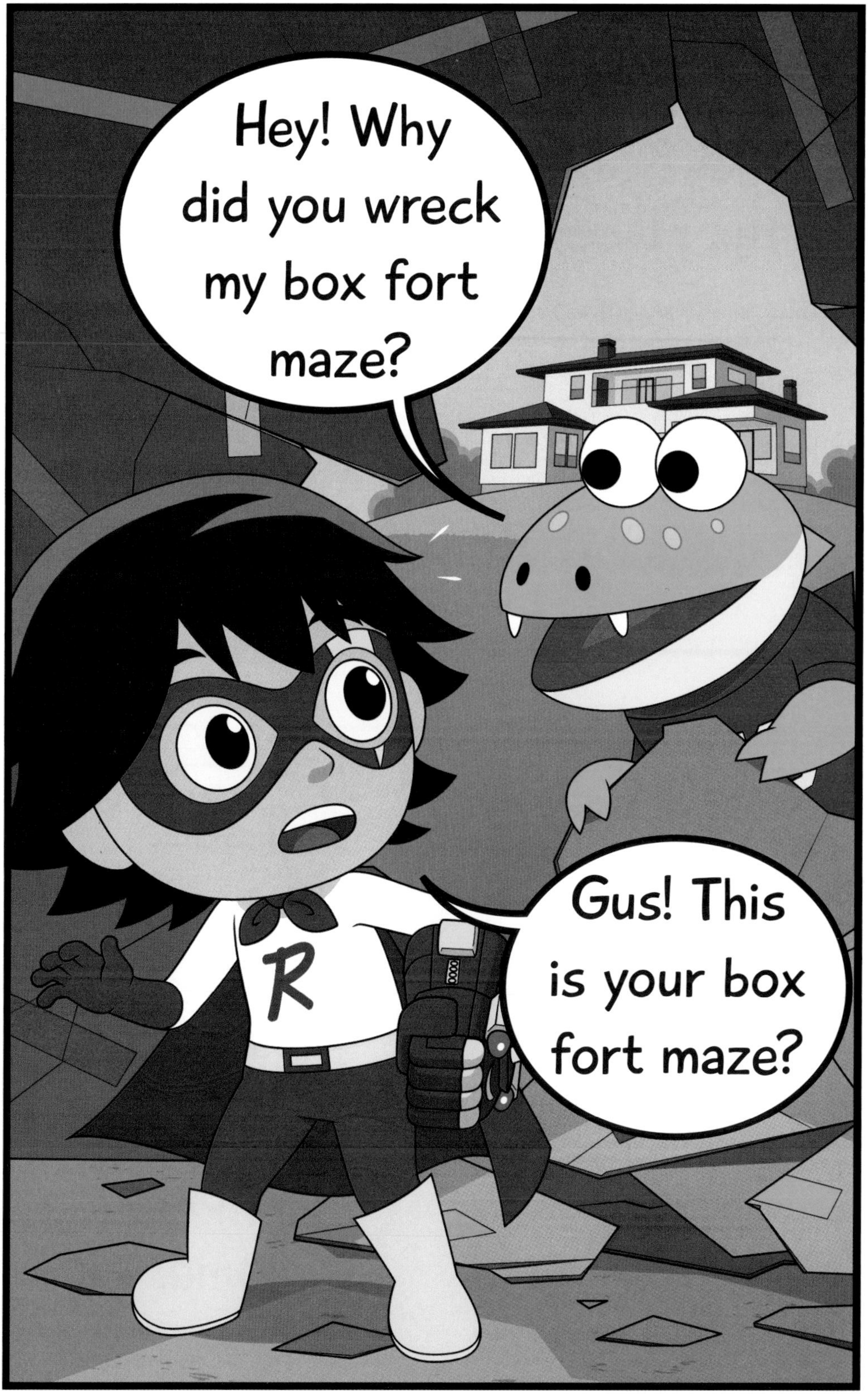
Hey! Why did you wreck my box fort maze?
Gus! This is your box fort maze?

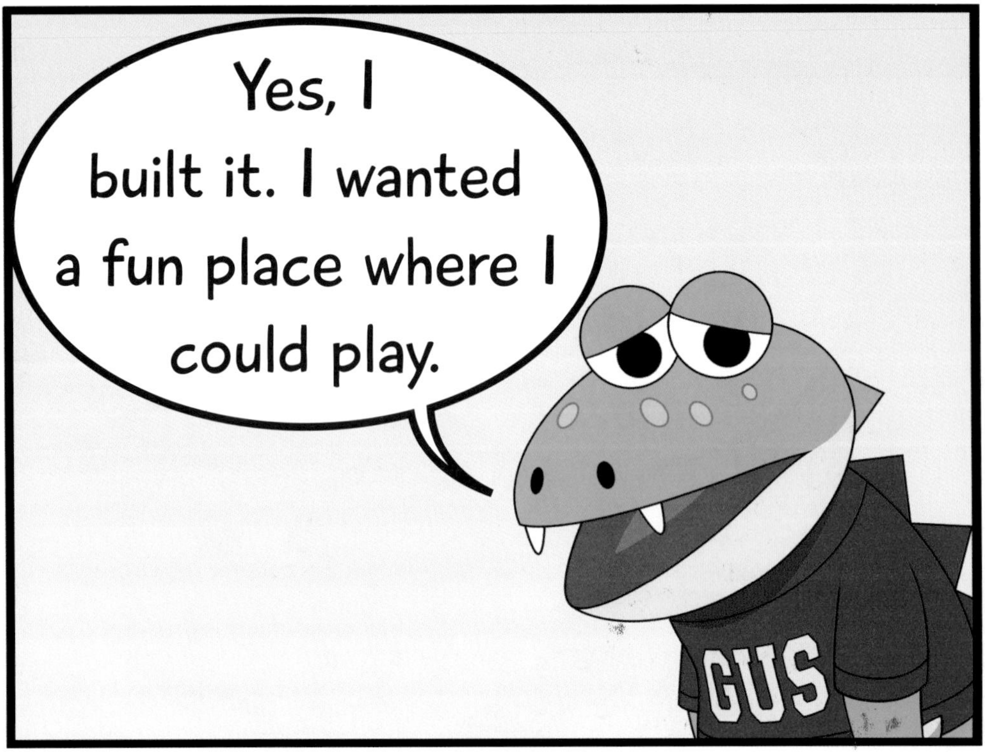
Yes, I built it. I wanted a fun place where I could play.
GUS

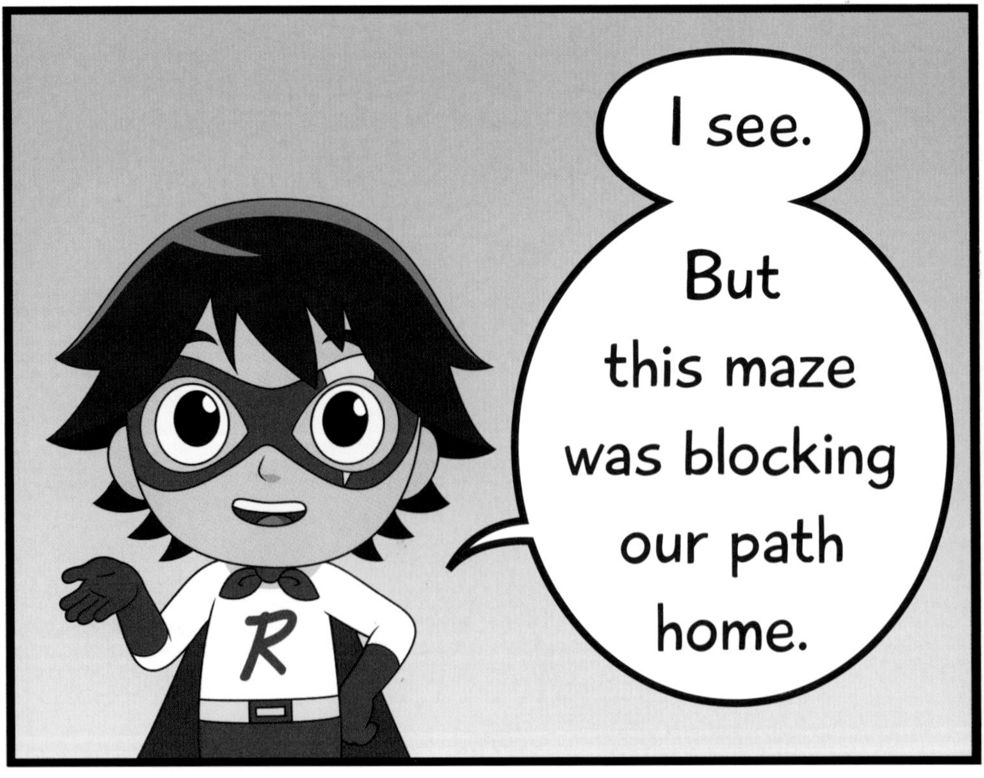
I see.
But this maze was blocking our path home.
R

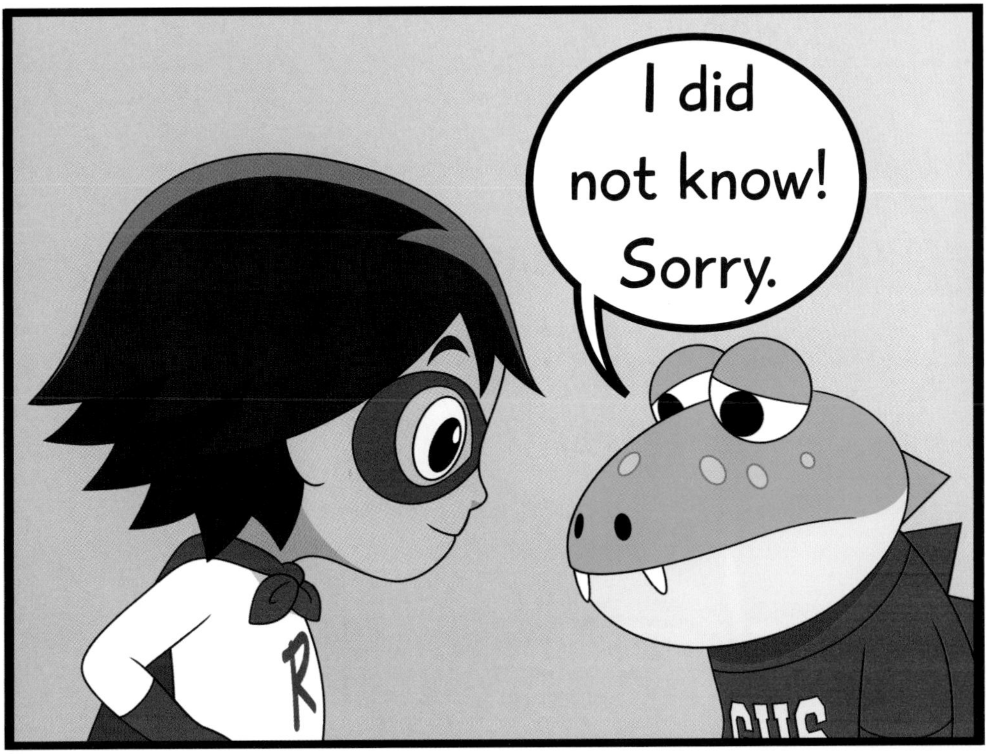
I did not know! Sorry.

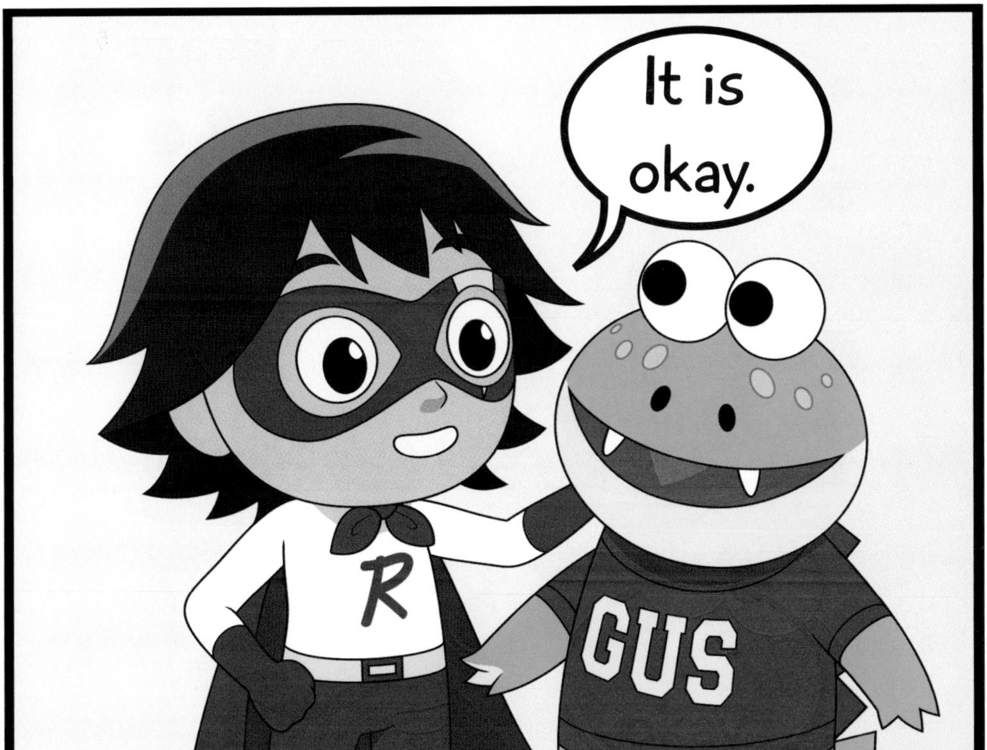
It is okay.
GUS

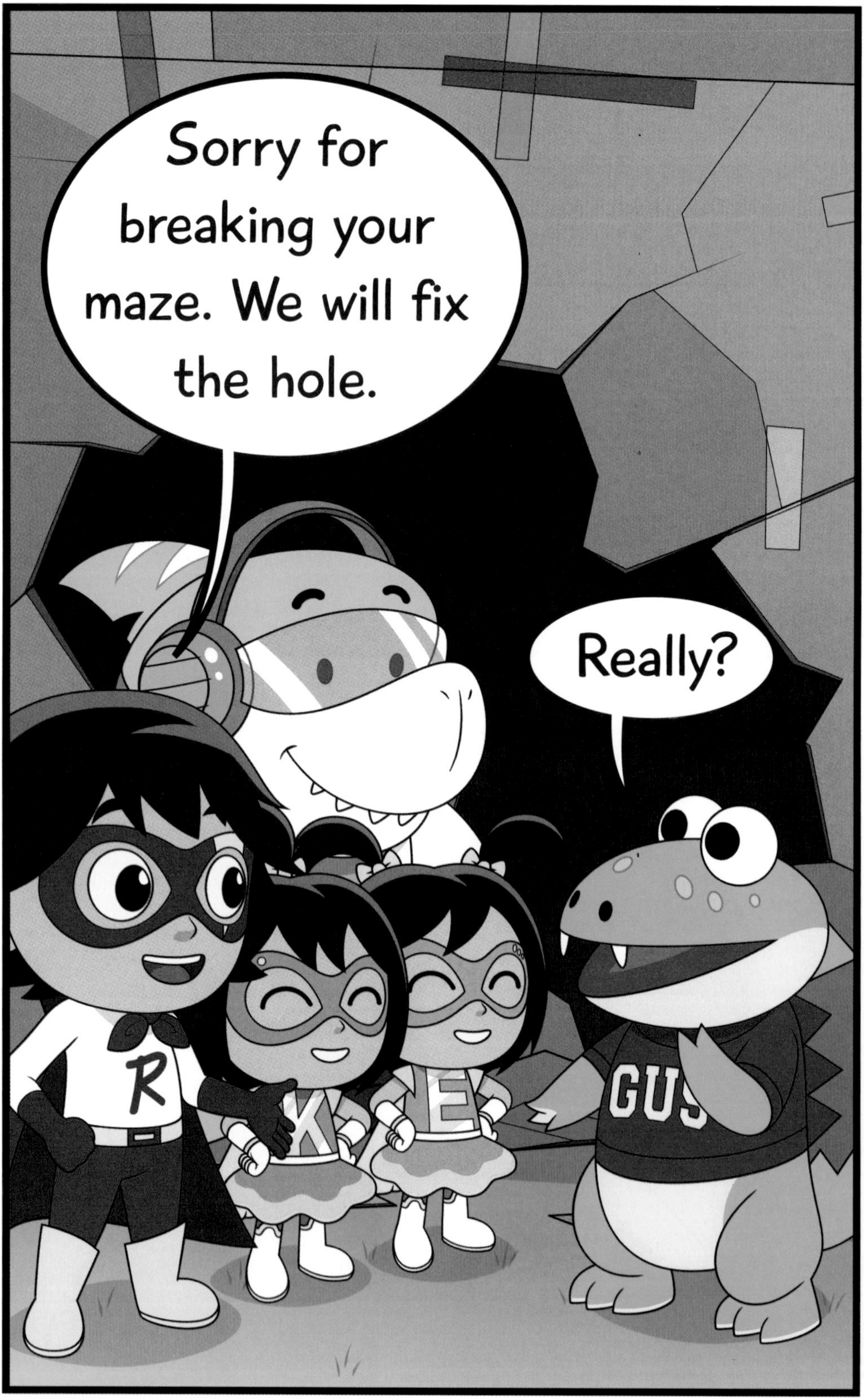
Sorry for breaking your maze. We will fix the hole.
Really?

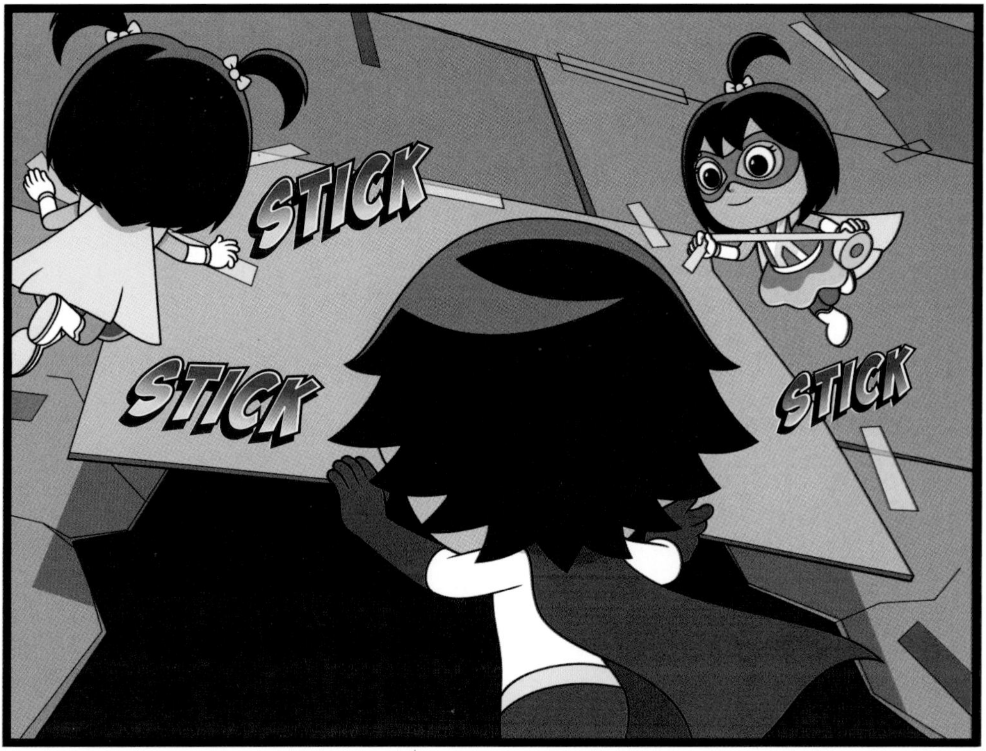
STICK
STICK
STICK

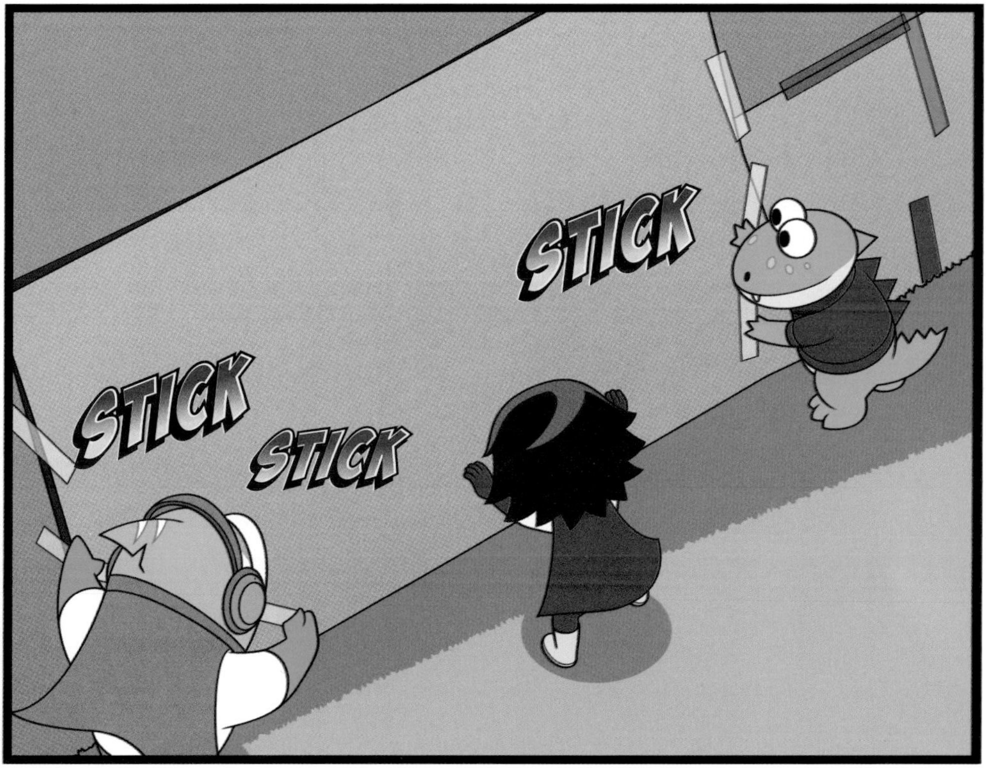
STICK
STICK
STICK

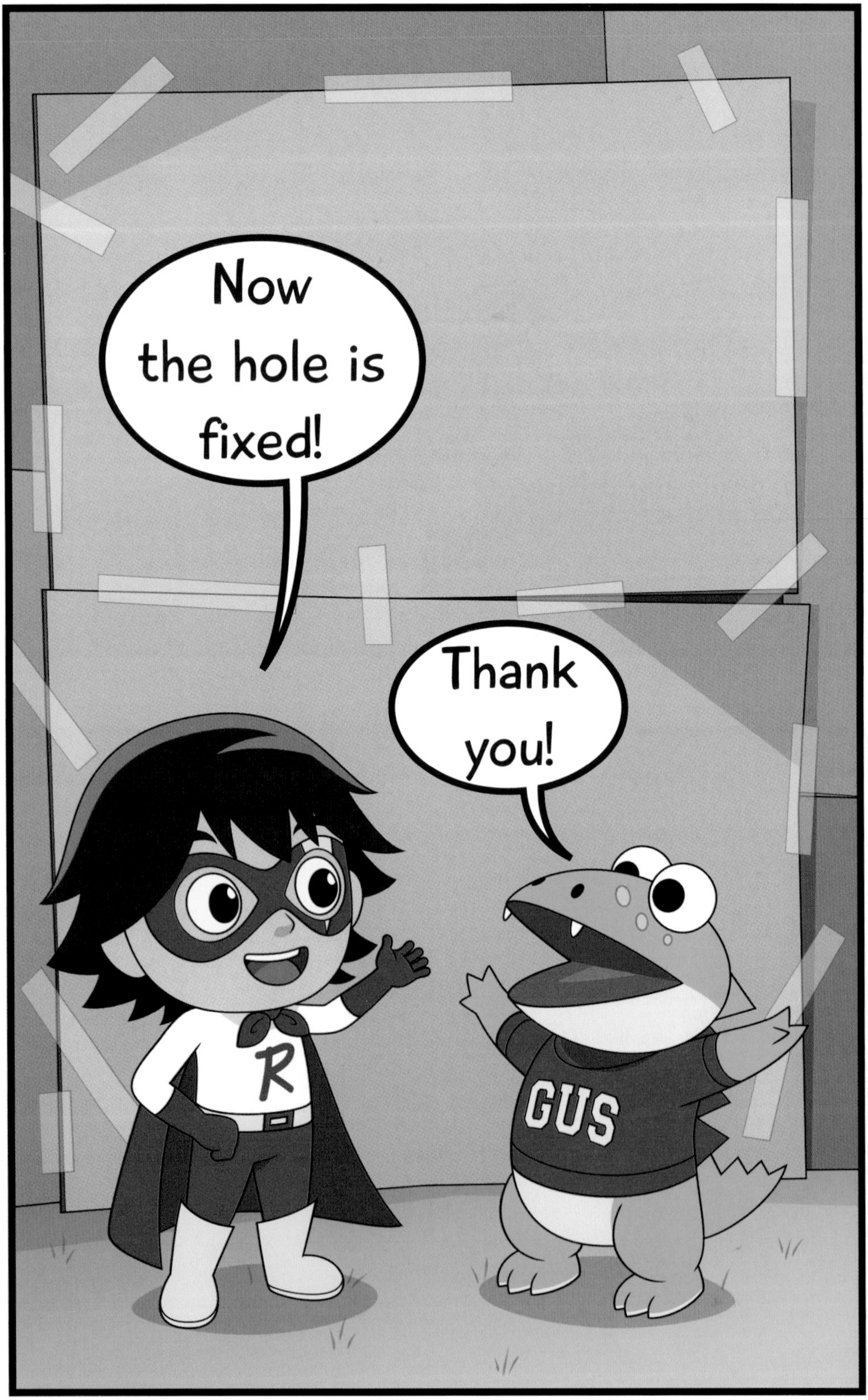
Now the hole is fixed!
Thank you!

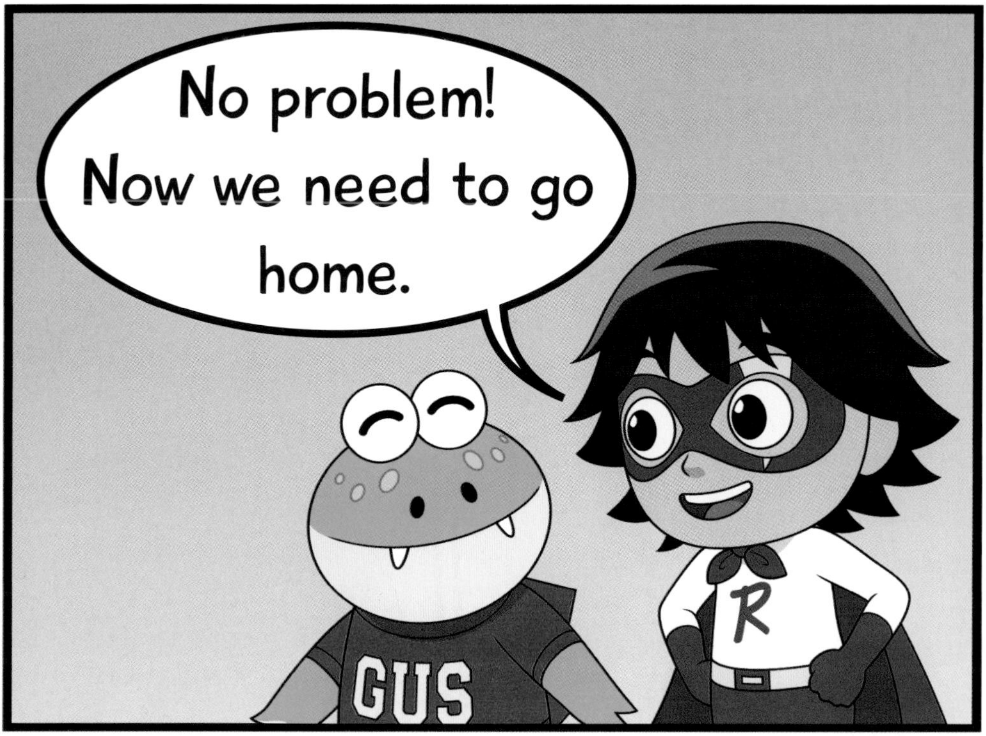
No problem! Now we need to go home.
GUS
R

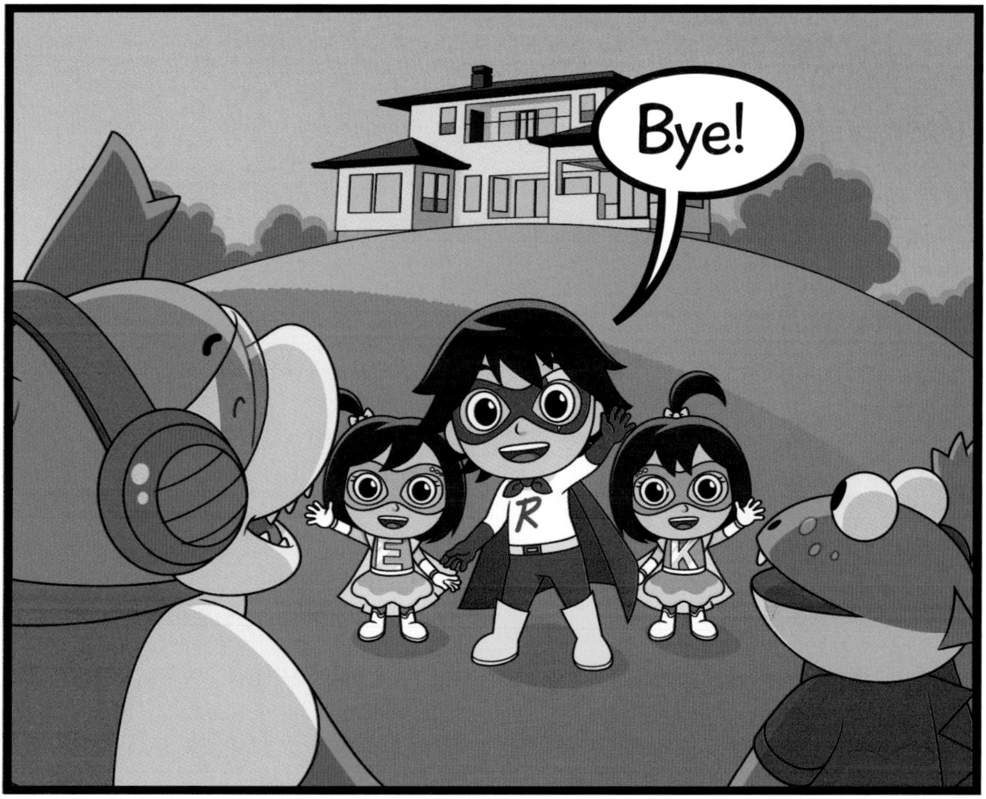
Bye!
E
R
K

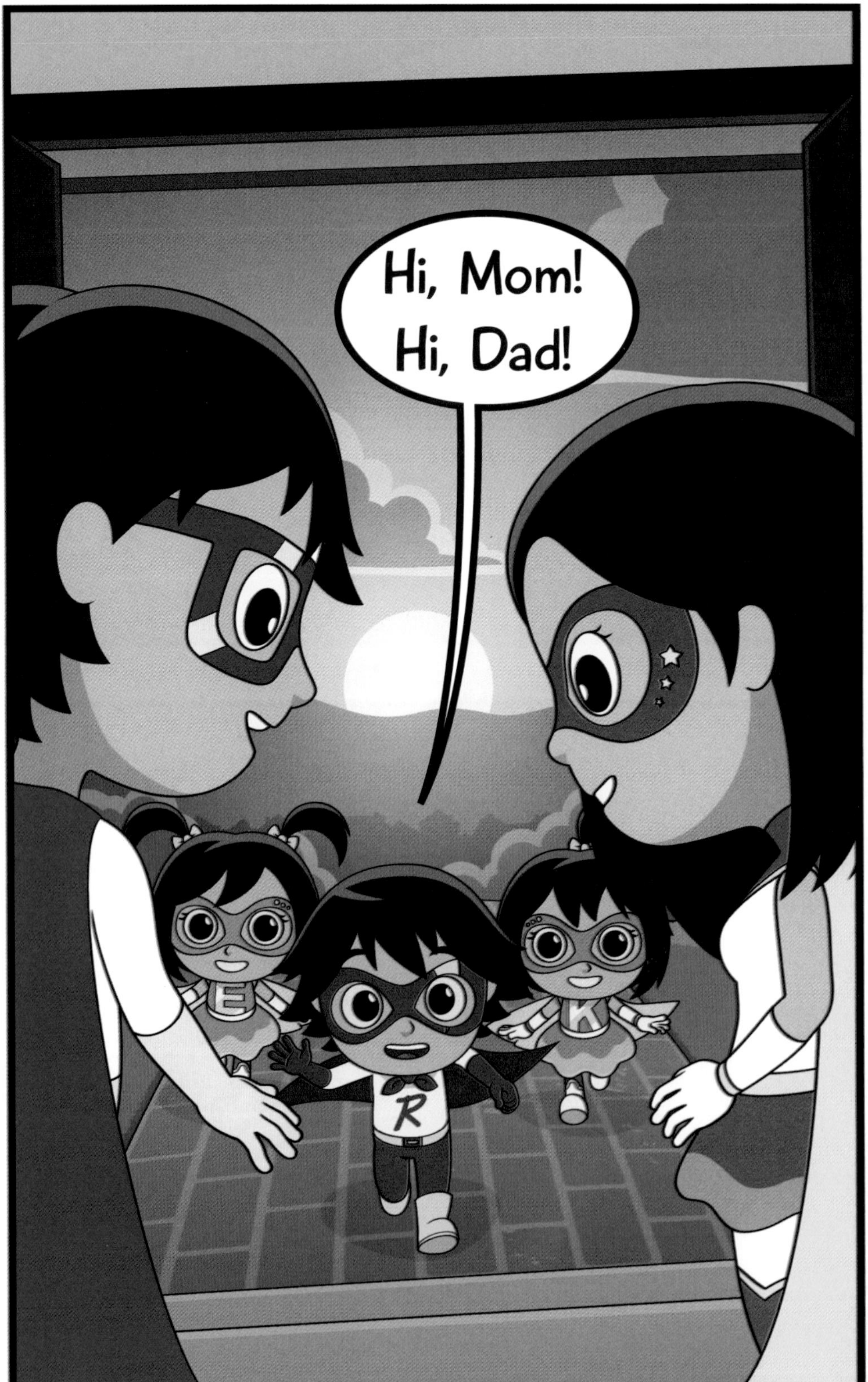
Hi, Mom!
Hi, Dad!

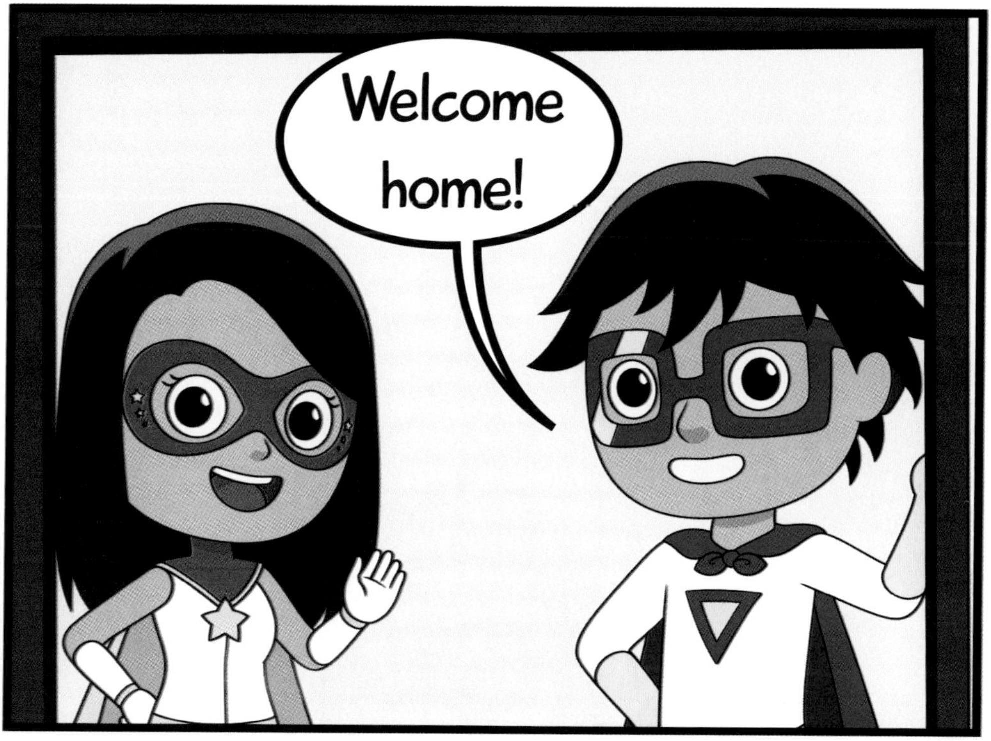
Welcome home!

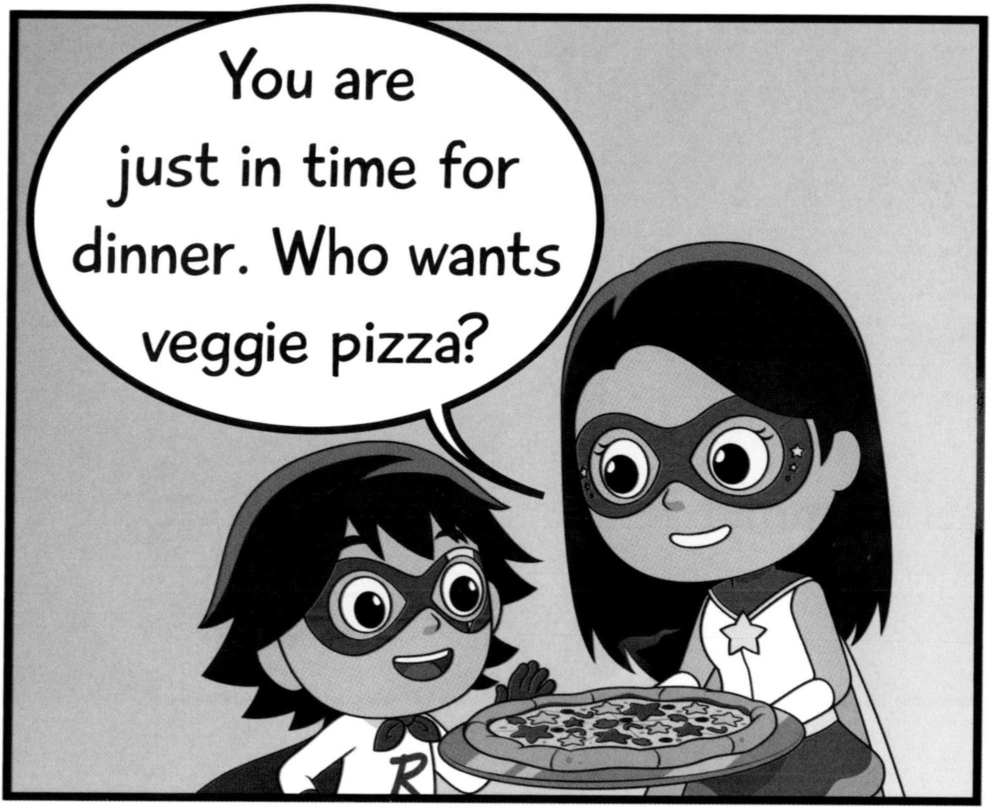
You are just in time for dinner. Who wants veggie pizza?

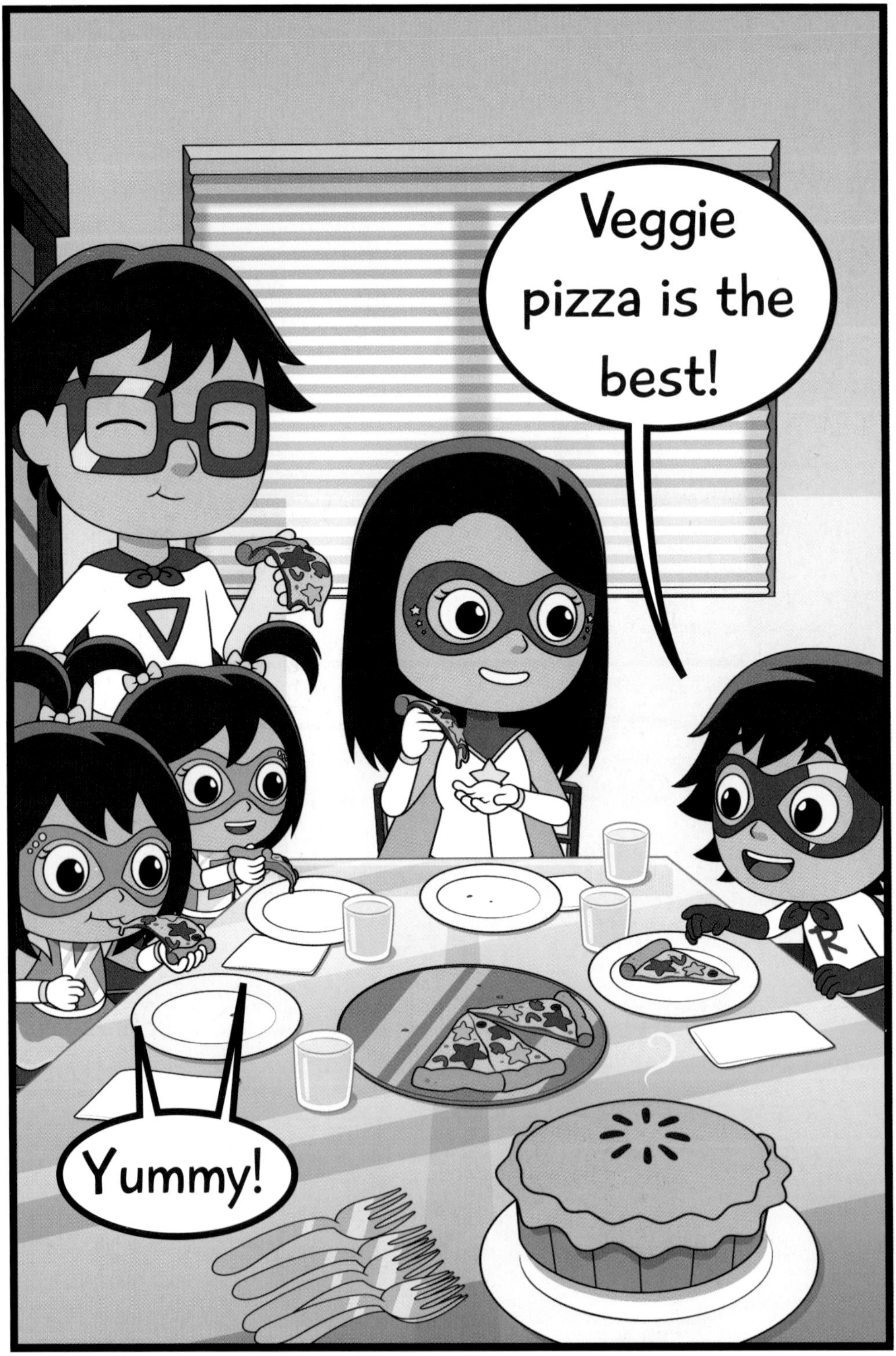
Veggie pizza is the best!
Yummy!

Red Titan has saved the day!